"KANDAR OF FERRANOZ, WILL YOU SELL YOUR SOUL TO SAVE YOUR LAND AND YOUR PEOPLE?"

Kandar stared at the sorcerer, in whose evil eyes a light of madness flared. A ghostly chill of fear crept through him. How much *would* he give to free his city from the spell that paralyzed it, and to save his family and his betrothed?

But there was no real choice. His sword, which had taken him this far, was useless against the necromancer. "Yes," he said firmly. "Anything that will save Dreaming Ferranoz, that will I do."

KANDAR

BY KENNETH BULMER

PAPERBACK LIBRARY

New York

PAPERBACK LIBRARY EDITION
First Printing: May, 1969

Paperback Library is a division of Coronet Communications, Inc. Its trademark, consisting of the words "Paperback Library" accompanied by an open book, is registered in the United States Patent Office. Coronet Communications, Inc., 315 Park Avenue South, New York, N.Y. 10010.

CONTENTS

Chapter One

Of the Ensorcellment that overcame Dreaming
Ferranoz and how Kandar sat down to read.

When the first ships of the wolf horde swept out of the red
dawnrise to raven down on Dreaming Ferranoz, Kandar
had long been closeted with his apparatus in his own secret retreat five miles outside the city walls.

He did not see those lean dark ships sliding down out of
the blood-red light over the ancient gray walls of Ferranoz. He did not hear the first screams, or the chirring of
the arrow storm or the surprised strident clangor as blade
met blade.

Wolf-like, the half-men leaped from their metal ships,
roaring a reckless challenge, their blades high, leaping
ferociously to slay and maim, battling for plunder and
rapine.

"This is not possible!" screamed a tall captain of the
guard. He screamed no more as a wolfman-driven javelin
pierced him through and his blood bubbled brightly over
gilded armor.

Frightened councilors scurried through the palace, their
slippers clack-clacking on marble flagstones and scuffling
on rare Sanghara rugs, to wake Pandin Heliodotus from
his wide silken bed. The Emperor awoke and understood.
His tired old face, deep-marked by the benign exercise of
power over fifty years, tautened with this fresh, this unex-
pected, this impossible, crisis. He hurried to a tall window
that commanded a broad perspective of towers and battlements and gleaming roofs. He saw the black smoke rising
evilly from the watchtowers.

"The last day has come," he said, and his gentle voice

betrayed the sorrow he felt. Pandin Heliodotus had been a mighty warrior in his youth, and although the iron strength might have left his limbs, it nerved his willpower and determination still. "Send for Quantoch—"

Before he could finish the command his son, the Prince Sheldion, appeared at the bedchamber door.

Sheldion wore full battle accoutrements, his gilded armor gleaming, the tall defiant plumes nodding from his helm. His hard face, brown with constant exercise and hunting in the sunshine, showed a tough and self-reliant strength. One day all Ferranoz would be his. No curs of wolfling half-men were going to deprive him of that golden heritage!

"Father—" he said, concern for the old man gentling his rough voice. "I have sent for Quantoch. But he is not to be found. Very early this morning he was seen slipping out—"

"By the south gate, I'll warrant!"

"Yes, father. He must have gone to see his brother Quarmeln—"

"And," said the Emperor heavily, "to plead once more with Kandar."

At the sound of the name the Prince Sheldion's face darkened.

"The city is attacked," he said, roughly, shaking himself out of unhappy thoughts. "The wolf horde have struck at the heart of the empire. They have flown in their metal ships clear across all the lands from the frontier. They are aided by a magic greater than ever they have used before—"

"Quantoch—"

"The court necromancer is absent in the hour of the city's peril! But whilst I have my true sword no wolfling will enter the palace—"

The dull and continuous rumbling from the city streets increased sharply. Individual sounds spurted up. The cry of a man mortally hurt. The clanging resonance as the bronze springs of a great catapult let fly. The clash of mail and harness, the gong-strokes of hand-to-hand combat, the sundering shriek of splitting metal.

"They are nearer! The fiends leap walls and battlements in their cursed magic flying ships! I must go, Father. I but

8

came to see you safe. My place is at the head of my men—"

"Go, my son, and may the spirit of the omnipotent Heliodotus go with you."

Saying this, Pandin Heliodotus, in the role of God-Emperor, signed the secret sign in the air before his son. Then he held his son's bare right hand, from which the mailed mitten dangled, in a brief farewell.

With a martial clangor of mailed feet the Prince Sheldion marched out.

From his tall window the God-Emperor watched the carnage, and his heart lay heavily in his breast.

Logic told him that the wolflings were being used.

The bright Empire of Akkar and its brightest jewel, the capital city of Ferranoz, had long resisted all efforts to destroy its wonder and life. From the Sea of Dreams to the west came corsairs and reavers; from the swamps and the ice floes of the south ranged fur-clad barbarians and outlaws, and from the encompassing lands and deserts and forests to north and east stole shadowy assassins and marched glittering armies of men and half-men, all, all those beings outside the pale of Akkar, bent on the destruction of the fairest civilization on Earth.

He looked down and saw the columned infantry of the Guard marching in ranked steadiness toward the conflict. But his spirit trembled. Of what avail swords and spears against the evident magic that had transported the wolf horde in slender metal ships through the air and over the centuries-old walls of Ferranoz?

Where was Quantoch? Orders had been given, and fleet chariots had sped in riven dust clouds southward toward Kandar's secret retreat. But the feeling of doom pervaded the air. Pandin Heliodotus found it difficult to draw breath. He doubted that even Quantoch's unrivaled mastery of the thaumaturgical arts could win the day for Bright Akkar and Dreaming Ferranoz.

The Emperor fretted and trembled and tried to bolster his iron-spirit with strong beliefs in victory but his evil premonition of disaster would not be shaken off.

Akkar had grown over the centuries, ever pushing outward with the light of civilization. Sometimes her frontiers had diminished as some petty lordling, cunning with the arts learned from Ferranoz itself, had momentarily carved himself out a kingdom; but then the outward tide of pacification had resumed. But now, now for some five centuries, the frontiers had remained static, save for a few inevitable local adjustments. The snarling of the barbarians had grown fiercer over the years. Pandin Heliodotus searched his own heart for a reason and could find none.

A sound on the marble floor brought his attention away from the evil sights and sounds outside and he turned to see King Shamrath enter, clutching his robe agitatedly about him. Not chronologically as old as the God-Emperor, King Shamrath wore his years less easily. His yellow-dyed beard and his drawn face alike betrayed the fear writhing in him, as he pulled that beard with one hand, dragging at his robe with the other. He staggered to an onyx chair and slumped, his lips trembling.

"It is the last of the Days," he said, breathily.

Pandin Heliodotus was not to be seen dejected before a lesser king, even if that king ruled a land in fee to Akkar, away on her southern borders, a buffer state long erected between the Empire and the blubber-eating barbarians of the south.

"It may be as you say, Shamrath, the last of the Days foretold to us by the Books. But we will meet whatever the dark fates have in store for us like men and like warriors!"

Shamrath swallowed. He peered up distractedly. "I saw the Crown Prince, going forth to battle, noble and proud and truly warlike; but I did not see your younger son—" Shamrath swallowed again. "I have sent Elthalee to the women's quarters; but—but—"

Thunder darkened the brow of the Emperor.

"Fear not, O king, that your granddaughter will not be marrying a man and a warrior!"

"No—you know me better than that, Pandin. We have been friends since our youth, and I am overjoyed that at last our houses will be joined. But this day every man of Akkar must fight!"

"Every man will!" And Pandin Heliodotus turned once more to the vista of battle.

King Shamrath joined him, and together the two old

men looked out on the battle that would decide perhaps for a thousand years the destiny of the Empire.

The Prince Sheldion jumped lithely down the marble steps of the palace that rose dominating the city. All about in the broad avenues and the narrow connecting streets flames flickered cruelly and black smoke rose against the morning sky. The sun would shine hotly today; yet the scenes on which it shed its rays would burn and smolder with a fierceness it could not know.

An armored groom struggled with his horses harnessed to his war chariot. Milk-white steeds from the far east, each one represented a fortune in jewels and gold. The four of them would ransom two petty kingdoms.

"Not today!" snapped Sheldion. He waved the grooms aside. "Street fighting is no place for a quadriga. Ho there, my warriors! Dismount, all!" He stared arrogantly forth on his personal chariot squadron.

Fifty chariots, all gilded and painted, all harnessed with matched steeds sleek and groomed in the morning light, fifty fighting machines with men armed with javelin and spear, sword and shield, they waited on the broad marble forecourt of the palace.

"Dismount!" shouted Sheldion. He snatched up the heart-shaped chariot shield, cunningly-shaped for quadriga work. He lifted his broadsword aloft. "Today we fight on the feet the good Lord Helios gave us!" He smiled proudly on his men. "This day will cure your corns!"

Dismounting, his men laughed at the crude joke. Avid for war, trained fighting men, they thirsted for action.

A waft of black smoke and an evil stench of burning gusted across the forecourt. Straight ahead, the Imperial Way stretched from the palace down `a series of wide steps, going straight across the center of the city toward the harbor and the sea. Halfway along, a knot of struggling men was being slowly pushed back as the wolflings fought their way toward the ultimate prize of their conquest.

"Form wedge!" shouted Sheldion.

Quickly the charioteers ran to form a triangular mass of men, spears leveled, shields up, the inner men ready with poised javelins.

Sheldion's driver, a gnarled and massive man clad in

11

thick leather armor, studded with bronze, took the second-larger chariot shield from its beckets above the gilded and finely-spoked wheels.

"I am your back today, master," he grunted.

Sheldion nodded. "Good Tojas, with your strength to guard me I fight as ten men."

All was ready. The wolflings down the Imperial Way had pushed nearer. Already the charioteers could see the white splodges of the infantry of the guard's faces. The infantry had turned. They were facing back. They were running.

With a firm and steady step the Prince Sheldion marched to the apex of the triangle. He positioned himself at the point of that armoured wedge. Tojas, blank-faced, grim and unforgiving, positioned himself to Sheldion's left and rear. There would be no sudden spear-thrust from that quarter to bother the prince.

Sheldion lifted his sword. The blade gleamed with a flash of white fire in the sunlight.

The blade swept down.

The mass of men swept forward at once in a jog-trot motion that would carry them through the ranks of any enemy.

Sandaled feet beat against the marble. Sweat dripped. Bronzed hands clasped spear haft and javelin, the heart-shaped chariot shields lifted high in hedgehog defense. The Charioteers of Ferranoz plunged forward.

A single thought pulsed in Sheldion's mind.

"We must fight on until Quantoch is found! Only Quantoch can save us against this evil magic!"

The infantry scattered. A howl of triumph arose from the wolflings. They raced forward, intent on cutting right through to the palace and all its treasures, its gold and jewels, its wines and plate, its women . . .

That breaking wave of gray bodies hurled squarely against the charioteers' flying wedge.

At once the clangor of arms, the shriek of dying men and half-men, the insane clamor of pitched battle racketed through the marbles and columns of the Imperial Way.

This was no exercise, no battle-maneuver, no well-contrived drill. This was red blood spurting, this was severed arms and heads bounding on the marble, this was gray ferocious shapes reeling back with the javelins protruding from gray-white bellies. At the apex of that triangle of death Sheldion wielded his brand like a god of myth, slaying any who ventured within the sweep of that deadly blade.

In that first shock the gray shapes struggled, hung an instant like a wave on shore, and then broke and reeled back, scattered, and fled.

Panting lightly, breathing under perfect control, his sword a reeking red brand, Sheldion led his men on.

A shadow flicked over the Imperial Way.

Sheldion glanced up. Sudden understanding hit him with a moment of horror; then he had himself under control again and was screaming orders to his men.

Over the heads of the Charioteers of Akkar a long evil metal shape hovered in the air. A hull shape, like the sleek galleys that plied the Sea of Dreams, supported on nothingness, held swimming in the empty air like an iridescent bubble, the ship swayed over them. From its sides poured forth the balefire, green globes of a fuming, bubbling substance that reeked with the charnel smeath of death. Where those globes of greenish light struck a man they clung like leeches, burning, dissolving, liquefying. In seconds the wedge shape had been smashed; charioteers fleeing away on every side to escape the burning and corroding balefire from above.

As they ran, the half-men closed in, their weapons ready. Sheldion saw his men cut down, saw the wolflings howling in savage cruel glee.

Those wolf-men sprouted a hard bristle of gray short-spined hair all over their bodies; their muzzles showed black-gummed, yellow-fanged; their eyes were red and evil and alight with the knowledge of hellfire. Raging victoriously, they slavered in for the kill. Surrounded by the gristly gray bodies, Sheldion and Tojas fought, back to back, their swords' white fire long since slimed with the grimmer hue of death.

Step by step, foot by foot, joined now by first one and then another of the sundered charioteers, they battled their way back toward the palace. The ship above them, the intelligences who guided her evidently confident in the destruction they had wrought, glided off to sow more balefire upon the city defenders.

"By Helios!" panted Sheldion. "What foul pit spewed forth these fiends?"

He cut down a leaping wolf shape and felt fangs rip at his shoulder. A blade licked from his side and the half-man fell away, half his head sliced, screeching. Again and again their swords stabbed in and out, again and again they rose and fell, and along that blood-bedabbled pathway they left a trail of wolfling corpses.

They had marched forth proudly in their wedge shape along this route only moments ago, confident in their power and strength; and now a rabble struggled desperately to bring back their prince alive.

The morning sunlight had still not attained its full power, shadows still lay a man's length from a man, and yet the city was fallen. So suddenly had this disaster overwhelmed Sheldion that he had had time only for the immediate fight. As his mightily muscled right arm rose and fell, stabbed and cut, as he hewed a pathway through the gristly gray wolfling bodies, he knew he must summon unearthly aid, Quantoch or no Quantoch.

"Cover me!" he snapped gustily at Tojas and the few others with them. They closed in around him. They knew what he was going to do, and he could sense the fear fresh in them.

Thaumaturgy as an art form was strictly reserved to the nobility. By virtue of the divine power vested in his father, the God-Emperor, the Prince Sheldion could partake also of the hidden knowledge of ancient times and deal with the shadowy realms of necromancy. Now he must put forth all his powers, as yet limited through youth, to defy these foul fiends from a deeper hell than any owned by Helios.

He began to form the incantation that would turn to a jelly the wolflings' bones below the knee, but stumbled over the first canto and had to cancel and start again. He knew the cunning grip on a javelin or a sword hilt better than this book-learning, but he struggled on, sweating and swallowing and gasping in the dust and the sunlight as the battle raged about.

He had reached the part where he said; ". . . and by Thothak and by Mumulak let the bone of their bones become less than bone and let the sinew of their sinews

14

become—" when the flung javelin took him in the collarbone. It had glanced off Tojas' shield, deflected by a sword blow as he cut down a half-man, and plunged a hairsbreadth away from the edge of Sheldion's neck armor. Most of the force had been taken off by Tojas' shield; yet the blow punished Sheldion with sickening force. He staggered and fell.

"Quickly now, lads!" snarled Tojas.

Heedless of the half-men now, Tojas bent, hoisted Sheldion. He turned like an ox and ran for the palace steps. Javelins clattered behind him. Three of the charioteers fell, screaming. Fleetly ran big lumbering Tojas, bearing his master on his back.

Then, summoned by the frantic call of Pandin Heliodotus, a line of archers, trim in their green and brown, appeared on the topmost palace step. A snapped command, the simultaneous twang of a score of bowstrings, the soundless sigh of fiercely-driven arrows—and twenty leaping wolflings curled gristly gray bodies about twenty shafts in their bellies.

"Hurry!" snapped the bowman captain. "Everywhere is lost. Survivors are pulling back to the palace—"

"Quantoch!" panted Tojas, lumbering up the steps beneath his burden from which the dark blood dropped. "Where is the magician!"

From his bedchamber Pandin Heliodotus had called for his armor. Chased and gilded, plate and mail, tall helm and cunningly contrived pauldrons, all his armor, all was brought and ranged on the rare Sanghara rugs. Of all that glittering array of war harness Pandin Heliodotus chose a plain steel mesh, plated as to chest and back, stark and brutal and efficient.

Stiffly he bent his joints to don that grim panoply.

Then he took up his good sword, the true blade Peveril, and essayed a cut or two. The old cunning had not left his arm. Solemnly, conscious of the momentousness of the occasion, Pandin Heliodotus, God-Emperor of all Akkar, stepped out onto the topmost step of his palace stairway, girt for battle, an old man, but not unworthy to be God-Emperor of all Akkar.

Ferranoz blazed to the skies.

A group of ordnance warriors were still operating their

15

ballista from a lonely tower flanking the palace gates. The twin to that tower had long since been pulled down to make way for a pleasant pleasure garden of roses and thyme and scarlet funley-flowers. Now, undreamed-of though it was, the old original tower would have been of more use than a pleasant pleasure garden.

The ballista thumped, and a rock flew to gong sweetly against the metal hull of a prowling metal ship of the air. Proudly, Pandin Heliodotus watched as his men fought to the last. Tojas carried the blood-streaming body of the Prince Sheldion past him. Smoke billowed down. The noise increased. Sheldion opened an indistinct eye.

"Father—" he said, weakly. He could say no more. There was nothing more of value to be said.

Pandin Heliodotus summoned to his aid all his hard-won knowledge of magic. He faced magic of a nature frightening and unholy, magic that could cram a hundred ravenous wolflings into a metal shell and hurl them clear across the frontiers of Akkar to burn and loot and kill in the Dreaming city of Ferranoz itself. Defiantly he put his right foot down on the topmost marble step. His left hand grasped with an old man's tremble the hilt of the true sword Peveril. He formed the opening phrases of the incantation that would wither the right arms of the enemies of Akkar.

He remembered well enough; but the holding of the conception in his mind was difficult, very difficult. He sought to grasp the enchantment entire, and bits kept slipping away, so that he was like a juggler with old and stiff joints trying to balance too many cups and plates at once. Grimly he strove to hold the spell. Grimly he strove to hurl all his arts of necromancy at the foul invaders of his city. Grimly he struggled—and grimly he failed.

"Quantoch!" he panted, despairingly holding his right hand into his side where a stitch had begun. "Quantoch!"

Once more he tried, and this time through some inner compulsion of his imperial being he held the incantation whole and entire for ten heartbeats.

The wolflings ravening up the palace steps against the archers and the remnants of the infantry of the guard and Sheldion's charioteers abruptly screamed, falling back. Swords and javelins clattered to the marble. Gray gristle

16

backs showed, as the wolflings ran. Each half-man for a hundred yards from Pandin Heliodotus had seen his own right arm wither and shrivel and become useless.

"The range is too short!" gasped the Emperor. Other wolflings ran up to take over the attack, another flying ship landed more attackers, and the spell was gone from Pandin Heliodotus' brain.

King Shamrath clutched his arm, shaking.

"Pandin! Pandin! They are attacking the women's quarters! All our troops are dead or fled!"

"Oh, Quantoch!" Pandin Heliodotus made the secret sign of blessing in the air. "Dreaming Ferranoz is doomed!"

When the first ships of the wolf horde swept out of the red dawnrise to raven down on Dreaming Ferranoz, Kandar had long been closeted with his apparatus in his own secret retreat five miles outside the city walls.

The room stretched long and narrow in the flank of a low mound, approached only by a single narrow track through thickets and guarded by a ponderous door of oak and bronze. Around the stone-buttressed walls ranked the empty niches where once had lain the moldering bones of long dead warrior-kings. Now the lights burned on complicated-looking twists of glass, retorts and phials, tiny ceramic-faced brick kilns and furnaces, bottles in row after row, clumsy arrangements of copper and iron and zinc.

"Faster, Maggra, faster!" Kandar fairly danced with excitement. Quarmeln, at his side, despite his experienced years, peered forth in delighted wonder.

The lithe muscles of Maggra's oiled body responded as he turned the handle faster and faster. Kandar's own body writhed in counterpoise with each revolution. Faster and faster whirled the great wheel.

"Keep it up, Maggra! Any minute now!"

Quarmeln nodded. Maggra sweated and bobbed. The wheel flew around between its supports. Decisively, Kandar pushed a lever.

From the wheel flew fat crackling sparks, great evil blue-green writhing phantom shapes of fire!

Dancing and stranding like ropes of flame, they coruscated for an instant between the wheel and the shining copper balls above Kandar's lever.

17

Then the eerie light died as Maggra released the handle and with a magnificent howl of sheer terror dived beneath the nearest table. There he stayed, hands over his head, trembling.

Kandar laughed.

"Maggra, Maggra! There is nothing here to fear, this is the light of science—"

Quarmeln nodded, his amusement forgotten.

"Indeed, there may be something to fear. This is not a power we can easily control. This is not subject to the thaumaturgical arts. My brother, Quantoch, knows what he is doing when he conjures a spell; but here, you and I, Kandar, we are experimenting in darkness."

A deep bass voice boomed from the doorway.

"And in the darkness will remain, O misguided fools!"

Striking his cabalistically decorated staff on the stone before him, Quantoch strode in. His glittering green and gold robe had been stitched and embroidered stiffly with magical symbols, thaumaturgical art, runes of repute. His tall conical cap brushed cobwebs from Kandar's dusty ceiling. Renowned throughout the Empire of Akkar, Quantoch's reputation had spread far to the east and north, striking shivers of terror into the hearts of those who would ravish the Empire. Now he frowned upon his twin brother.

"Quarmeln! You lead the young prince astray with your foolishness! Science is worthless in this modern world! Only the magical arts can prevail! Of what use your pretty blue sparks against a spell—thus!"

In a sudden galvanic action the wheel began to spin of itself. Round gleamed the spokes like a lensed eye. A lurid yellow fire began to send wavering streamers out from the circumference of the wheel, and yet the wheel remained unconsumed.

"That is the spell of the Unburning Fire," remarked Quantoch. "That, I can control."

Kandar resigned himself to another lecture. The twin brothers would argue until the sun set. All he knew was that he could never seem to remember any useful spells, and he didn't feel inclined to carry with him everywhere he went, as Quantoch did, an immense tome of arcane lore. That dragonskin-bound book hung now from Quan-

18

toch's side chained by golden chains, never to be parted from him until he resigned his position as Priest-Magician to the Empire. Kandar sighed.

"Look at this young man," thundered Quantoch. "He can use a sword more skillfully than anyone in the Empire. Only his brother Sheldion can hurl a javelin more cunningly. And yet, here he is crouched in a dark room playing with useless toys when he should be out in the fresh air, exercising, or with me, learning his spells!"

"He is of a new breed, brother," said Quarmeln mildly. He wore a plain off-white smock, having said that the gorgeous symbolism of magic would not do for the sterner disciplines of science. "The Emperor's third marriage came late in life—the tragedies of his first two marriages do not concern us. But Kandar is a man who will make his mark upon the world—"

"And he cannot do that without a few spells in his head."

"But I need to learn about the new knowledge!" protested Kandar with his quick bubbling eagerness. His width of shoulder and lean ranginess seemed somehow camouflaged by his student manner; his very toughness melted before his impetuous search for the new learning.

"Leave this so-called science to the fools who dabble in it, lad!" Quantoch sounded absolutely confident. "You can trust arts of thaumaturgy—" Here he slapped the ponderous dragonskin-bound tome at his waist— "In here are writ the secrets that keep Ferranoz and Akkar safe, and the inspired knowledge to undo our foes!"

As his words rang in the dark air of the underground room, the oak and bronze door thundered open and two charioteers stumbled in, distraught, their faces ghastly with the horrors they had witnessed.

Their news drove all thoughts save the single one of fighting for his city from Kandar's brain. He grasped his sword, the true blade Skullskelper, snatched it from the scabbard by the door, and with it naked in his hand rushed from his secret retreat. The others followed. The chariot horses stood, stamping and blowing after their mad dash from the city. Not recking the cost, Kandar bounded aboard the nearest quadriga, lashed the horses, and in a wide spraying of loose stones clattered in a tight circle and back up the narrow path. His left hand tightened on the reins, his right firmed down over Skullskelper's hilt.

All his blood beat and sang to the challenge of the moment. Foremost among the youth of the city for strength and skill in combat, he had yet to taste his first draught of battle, yet to drink the heady wine of war.

The horses galloped as though they, too, sensed the gravity and occasion of the moment. A city burned and an Empire fell, yet still her warriors would fight on.

The chariots clattered out onto a wide plain of tall grass whereon the horses of the city disported themselves and grew sleek and well-fed. Cultivation of the soil had not been permitted here. Ahead now, clearly visible in the morning air, Ferranoz burned.

Kandar drew in his breath with a sharp gasp of understanding. The charioteers had not lied. He could see the darting dots swooping like evil vultures above the ramparts of the city. They must be ships—but how? How could a thing as heavy and massive as a ship—and a metal ship at that!—be supported in thin air? Only necromancy could do that, a magic as powerful as the enchantments sealed in Quantoch's book.

For Quantoch the understanding came that his hour of greatest trial had begun. This was the ultimate test for which his life had prepared him.

Already, as his twin brother handled the reins of the four horses and the chariot thundered across the plain, Quantoch crouched with his somber tome open, mumbling preparatory spells to himself. And a great horror came upon him, so that he glared out across the plain at the Dreaming city of Ferranoz, and his eyes revealed a knowledge almost too powerful even for his wizard-strengthened brain.

"There are mighty warlocks," he said in a whisper, so that Quarmeln barely heard him over the clash of hooves and the spring and groan of the lunging chariot. "Strange and uncanny spells have been woven for the destruction of Ferranoz and all Akkar!"

His brother glanced down. "Better for us had we listened to the wisdom of science—"

"Cease your babbling!" Quantoch's frame visibly swelled as he struggled to pull himself up. He clasped the

20

chariot rail. He stared out and up, and on his face a look of majesty and power radiated the promise of uncanny battle to come. "This is work for necromancers!"

Glancing quickly back, Kandar saw Quantoch standing in that pose of regal power, saw his uplifted, transfigured face, and knew with a little shiver in his spirit that the wizard was locked in a conflict invisible save for its results.

Ahead of them now the pall of smoke blew low over the ground. Flames shot up from towers and castles. All the fair face of Ferranoz was being ruined and despoiled. A metal ship skimmed low over the ground, flying just ahead of the roiling cloud of smoke. Cinders flew to light tiny blazes in the tall grass. The ship shuddered. In her side a great hole had been battered by a stone from a catapult. She drifted low and hesitated, then began to swing aimlessly. Kandar could see the wolflings running about the decks, clambering on ladders, collecting their loot, preparing to abandon ship.

"At least one of the accursed ships has paid a price!" said Kandar, lifting his sword.

The ship grounded athwart his road. The wolflings ignored his chariot and began to run across the plain toward a second ship, waving their arms and howling.

Among the gristly gray hides and the swart, brass-nailed armor, a flash of white flesh drew all Kandar's attention. He hauled back on the reins.

"By Helios!" he said. "They have attacked the women's quarters—and—" Suddenly, as though stricken by a flying arrow, he peered closer. "Elthalee!"

He was scarcely conscious of flicking the reins, of sending the chariot into headlong motion. The drumming hooves blended to the creak of wood and the jarring bounce of unsprung wheels. Two of the half-men carried Elthalee between them, quarreling. One pushed irritably at the other, who replied, stabbing the wolfling deeply in the throat. Victorious in this fierce internecine squabble, the wolfling grasped Elthalee tightly to him and began to run on.

The majority of the wolflings had reached the second ship, looming dim at the hazy edges of the smoke bank, and were swarming aboard. The tussle had delayed the wolfman carrying Elthalee. Kandar's four dynamic horses carried his chariot like a hurricane blast.

In the second chariot Quantoch put forth all his magic powers.

"They are mighty and evil, strange and fearsome powers that have ensorcelled the wolf horde, bringing them here in metal ships that fly, setting them to destroy all Dreaming Ferranoz." Foam appeared on his lips. He lifted his arms, balancing in the chariot as Quarmeln swung it around to a standstill to watch Kandar.

"Fly, O evil powers! Flee, you scorpions of the nether hells! By all the bright realm of Helios, begone!"

Sweat burst out all over the lined face. Quantoch groaned as the agony seized his brain and encircled his head with bands of iron and fire. Grimly he parted his lips, forcing out the words, grinding them through his teeth as a dishonest miller grinds his neighbor's corn.

"I command you to negate yourselves! Still, still! Stand rooted!" The struggle reached a crescendo, invisible, omnipotent, all-pervasive. "They will not go, they will not stand!" groaned Quantoch. His arms shook as the trees of the forest shake when Apsalothoc stalks at midnight.

Suddenly Quarmeln screamed, pointing at the city, his eyes wide with shock. "Look! Oh, my brother, you have accomplished something—but—but—"

Over the fair city of Dreaming Ferranoz rose black smoke and shot stabs of burning flame. But now that smoke remained as though frozen, unmoving, still. Stabs of flame revealed their inner lacy structure, unmoving, undying, unwavering. Nothing moved in Ferranoz. A wolfling stood rooted in the act of slaying an old woman; an infantryman of the guard stood poised back on his heel, his arm up with the javelin pointed, off balance and untoppling; a charioteer hung from his harness, upside down, his throat still half-slit by the fangs of a grinning wolfling; a great mass of stone hung motionlessly in the air ten yards from the unmoving cup of a catapult.

Choking, coughing, holding his throat and his forehead, Quantoch slumped to the floor of the chariot.

"What is it, brother?" demanded Quarmeln, querulously.

"I have heard," breathed Quantoch, painfully. "I have

22

heard, and it is written in the infamous volume called *The Ochre Scroll,* that two exactly equal sorcerers if matched can produce stasis. That is what happened. My arts and their black powers canceled out, and now Dreaming Ferranoz dreams in very truth!"

The silent city puzzled Kandar for a moment; but he could see the white limbs of Elthalee, his betrothed, struggling as she futilely beat her clenched fists against the gristly gray hide of the wolfling. He urged the horses on, flicking the reins over their sleek straining backs.

Skullskelper he laid on the floor of the chariot, having no scabbard, and he drew a javelin from the rack. He poised the slim haft. The cast was not difficult; but he dare not risk it yet. The wolfman bounded on with his prize, howling to his comrades to wait. The chariot thundered after him.

Evilly, like a signal from the gates of hell, a green globe of balefire curved out from the waiting ship. It arched in a perfect trajectory that would end on the chariot and on Kandar.

With a wild cry he leaped from the bounding chariot, hitting on a shoulder and rolling over and over, the stinking breath of the charnel house in his nostrils as the balefire burned the chariot to smoking ashes. Released, the four horses rushed crazily into the distance.

Kandar shoved up on a knee. Miraculously, he still grasped the javelin, from which two feet or so had been snapped as he rolled. He stood, poised, lifted his arm, aimed, threw.

Only the Prince Sheldion could have equaled that cast, and it is doubtful if even he could have bettered it. The keen blade drove deeply into the wolfling's side. But although Kandar's aim had been true, the fall from the chariot, his desperate resolve, his urgency, had combined to overpower his arm. He had thrown too forcefully. Clean through the half-man clove the javelin head; reddened, it issued from his ribs to plunge on into the soft white skin and flesh of the girl he clasped so cruelly. As the wolfling screamed his last agony and fell, so an echoing scream from Elthalee chilled the blood in Kandar's veins and drove him crazily forward.

"Elthalee!"

He kicked the wolfling body uncaring as he tenderly broke the javelin haft blasphemously joining those two bodies. She was not dead. Not yet, at least. With the javelin head deep in her side and the bright blood pulsing ominously, she could still open her eyes and look bravely and lovingly at him.

"Kandar—my prince—"

He could not speak. The rattle of chariot wheels and the stamp of horses' hooves told him that the twin brothers had reached the scene of the tragedy. He cradled the body of the girl he had been chosen to wed, who had been chosen to wed him, and he believed then that he loved her.

"Do not blame—blame yourself, my prince." Her eyes opened their cornflower blue to stare into his own slate-gray eyes. "I but wish you had pierced me with another weapon." She coughed, and blood dribbled rawly down her chin. Kandar wiped it away.

"Elthalee, forgive me—"

"The city!" said Quarmeln, touching Kandar's shoulder.

"My bride-to-be is dying!" said Kandar in a harsh and cruel voice. "Leave me be, let the city die also."

"But, my prince," faltered Quarmeln, "my brother has wrought a fearful wonder."

"A strange and wonderful outcome," boomed Quantoch. "And my arts tell me that all is not lost yet! Come, Kandar, young prince, Lion of Akkar! Lift your affianced bride! We must hurry with her into the city!"

"But—" gasped Quarmeln.

Dimly, Kandar understood. He lifted Elthalee tenderly.

"The city is under a spell," he nodded. "Nothing moves, so nothing dies. Elthalee, there, will not die!"

"Just so," said Quantoch. "Until my arts can unravel this knot. Until I can find the requisite secret powers, the hidden mysteries, once again to set in motion all the proud life of Dreaming Ferranoz!"

"And in that time," said Kandar, "we can so arrange events that no lives of men need be lost. And we can bring the greatest doctors of all Akkar to tend Elthalee—yes, yes, by Helios!" he breathed, turning in radiant joy on the necromancer. "I believe it can be done!"

24

"Then let us hurry before she bleeds herself to death inside."

The chariot carrying the four of them jounced over the Plain of Steeds to the city. Quarmeln at last, with a sideways glance at his brother, said, "One must carry Elthalee into the city—and that one, too, will remain forever motionless and—"

"Not forever, O my brother, you were ever a fool!" snapped Quantoch. "With my arts I shall—"

"I know," cut in Quarmeln with a quietness that silenced Quantoch. "I shall take her in. For I am the only one. You, my imperious brother, are needed to compound your black arts, and you, my proud prince of Akkar, are needed to roam the world in search of those hidden mysteries that Quantoch must have. I"—here Quarmeln looked down at the chariot floor—"I am but a poor man trying to understand the secrets of our life. That can wait."

It was not said easily.

"Thank you, Quarmeln. You are a true friend. Now, let us hurry—"

The chariot jounced towards the ensorcelled city of Ferranoz.

From that proud capital of Akkar, apart from the party with Kandar and the prisoners taken by the wolf horde, only three men and a girl, reeling from an evil tavern, and one other, escaped. The rest of those many thousands remained petrified.

Hanging motionless in the air, and glimpsed between the unmoving banks of smoke, the metal flying ships of the wolf horde also remained a part of that static drama.

Pandin Heliodotus, defiant at the head of the remnants of his palace guard, the Prince Sheldion, carried sorely wounded by his charioteers, King Shamrath, pale and distraught within the palace walls, these, too, remained rigid and unmoving beneath the clash of spells.

Kandar watched his old mentor carry the girl to whom he had been betrothed into the city. Quarmeln walked proudly, firmly, carrying his precious burden as an offering is carried to Helios on his day. They vanished within the ancient walls.

"And now, Kandar, Lion of Akkar, last remaining

scion of the ensorcelled city of Ferranoz," spoke Quantoch the necromancer, "we have work to do. In this volume, all that I have left to me of my vast thaumaturgical library, in this book, *The Thaumalogicon*, are to be found the sources of the mysteries I must know, dark and dreadful secrets even I, Quantoch, have never probed."

"I am ready," said Kandar, simply.

"Then we will begin," said Quantoch. And he opened the volume at the first page.

Chapter Two

Of the Sundering of The Thaumalogicon.

Grim and dark were the secrets contained in that dragonskin-bound tome. The wisdom of the past gathered and distilled through the keen minds of mighty men had been written down and bound up and locked away on parchment culled from the fair skins of slain virgins.

Now Quantoch moved the ancient pages with care.

His face showed an absorbed concentration that Kandar found sobering, a stark reminder that the forces with which they dealt could maim and kill, if not handled according to the rules and rites prescribed. The parchment rustled ominously.

Away over the Plain of Steeds the ensorcelled city of Ferranoz burned and smoked without movement, without stir, the flames held and checked and undevouring.

"Even I," said Quantoch softly, "Even I, with all my knowledge, have not dared uncover many of the inner mysteries of *The Thaumalogicon*."

He turned pages reverently.

"Can you find the secret knowledge we must know?" asked Kandar tensely.

26

The court necromancer mumbled to himself as he slowly turned the pages, fragments of the names of spells and enchantments slipping raggedly from his withered lips. His beard moved waveringly, he licked his lips, he looked old and frail, a bent old man seeking mysteries that perhaps were never meant for mortal eye.

"You were never an enthusiastic learner, Kandar," grumbled Quantoch. "There is so much I could have taught you, so much you must know now—If only I had the infamous volume called *The Ochre Scroll!*

"Was there never a copy in the court library—?"

Quantoch chuckled evilly. "The world is coming to an end, and the bright Empire of Akkar is doomed—so I do not mind telling you that there never was a copy of *The Ochre Scroll* in the library."

Kandar looked resentful. "On two counts, Quantoch, on two counts I challenge you! You always pretended you had access to that devilish knowledge—"

"Yes, yes, lad. And the other count?"

"Why, the Empire of Akkar is not doomed! I shall seek for the information you require, we can break the stasis, we can defeat whatever intelligences are controlling the wolflings!"

"Bravely spoken, by Helios!"

A long metal ship ghosted around the curve of the petrified smoke cloud from ensorcelled Ferranoz.

Quantoch cocked an evil eye at it.

Kandar, quickly, said; "They will take us for more of the dead if we do not move."

The ship sailed silently on, a slender spear of destruction in the sunlight.

Gray-gristle wolfmen thronged her decks, their weapons a glitter. Slowly she turned, circling the barren city.

"They're puzzled," said Quantoch. "They do not yet understand what has happened. But soon—soon—"

"*The Ochre Scroll!*" snapped Kandar impatiently. "Who had a copy? Where is one to be found? We do not have much time—"

Quantoch chuckled his evil chuckle again. "Not so, O my valiant Prince Kandar, Lion of Akkar, last scion of Dreaming Ferranoz! We have all the time in the world, for nothing will age in Ferranoz while we are gone!"

"Then what did you mean by 'soon—soon'?"

"Soon the intelligences who have brought this disaster on us will understand what has happened. Then they, too, will seek to unbalance the balance, to tip the scales once more into motion. But they can do nothing. I know. A superior knowledge is needed now."

"Yes. *The Ochre Scroll*—"

"That is but one book. We need *The Ochre Scroll*, which, together with *The Umbre Testament* and *The Thaumalogicon* makes up the infamous *Trilogos Damnae*, the horrendous *Trilogy of the Damned*."

As he spoke the words a little duststorm gusted. A whirl of dust motes there on the Plain of Steeds gyrated about them like a phantom shroud. As quickly as it sprang up it died.

Kandar shivered.

"Even the names have strange powers," whispered Quantoch.

He fingered his own copy of *The Thaumalogicon* again.

"You must learn the enchantments needful, Kandar. The only man I know who possesses a copy of the *Scroll* is Thurdur the Cunning. For many years I have sought to make him part with it; but it gives him a power in his own land commensurate with mine here."

"Where is he?" demanded Kandar, alight with ardor, impatient to be off. "Give me directions and I will bring the *Scroll!*"

"Far north, far beyond the confines of the Empire of Akkar. I have corresponded with Thurdur—by means you would not comprehend—and by mortal messenger. He dwells many leagues away where the writ of Akkar does not run."

Bubbling anger boiled in Kandar. He had known Quantoch all his life, had looked up to him for many years as the wisest of all men, until he had realized Quantoch's twin brother, Quarmeln, with his calm zeal for the true light of science, was the greater man; but he had never known the court necromancer so lost, so broken, as this.

There on the Plain of Steeds with his burning city held in a magical petrification and the wolfling hordes prowling in their enchanted metal flying ships, Kandar Heliodotus,

Prince of Akkar, made another long step forward in his development. Gently he reached down and lifted the thaumaturgical tome against the golden chains. He pointed to a page heading: "Of the liquefaction of an enemy's legs, both below the knee and above, together with the jellification of the kneecap."

Gently he said: "That is a useful spell, Quantoch. I remember Sheldion told me of it. Shall we begin?"

The bubbling anger had evaporated; the screaming need to burst into violent action had been forcibly channeled into this sober search for help in the coming battles to find the answers to the mysteries they must know.

"Yes, yes," said Quantoch, oblivious to the change in tone of the young prince. "That indeed is useful. So are the other enchantments of like nature. You must learn them all by rote." He scuffed the pages with an absent yet impatient gesture. "Yet there are more significant mysteries, greater enchantments, here."

Kandar had not ever in his life missed noticing the end section of the book's golden hasp and lock, a full third of the pages forever under lock and key. He had never seen that section opened.

Now, with a tremble he could not still in his fingers, the court necromancer lifted a thin silver key from its hiding place, pulling it up on its silver chain from beneath his gold and green robe.

He made three tries before he could insert the key in the lock.

He glanced up at Kandar, standing tautly over him.

The Trilogos Damnae!" whispered Quantoch.

He turned the key in the lock.

Just what Kandar expected he could not have said.

A sudden burst of flame? A great gust of smoke and the frowning appearance of a genie? A swarm of bats with bloody fangs fluttering from the withered pages?

The book opened with a groan.

"Here," said Quantoch. "I have read this section once and then locked it up tightly again. Tightly! It is awesome knowledge—"

Kandar read: "Of the requisite means of retaining the spirit of a man slain in battle by your own hand."

29

"No," whispered Quantoch, "I have never slain a man in battle, in the red roaring madness of physical combat—"

A page turned.

Kandar read: "Of Kholokova and Sassilinja, their various apparations, powers and characters, and of the only sure way of retaining the senses."

"All this," said Quantoch, "all this, Kandar, Lion of Akkar, you must learn. For you will be pitted against powers—"

He broke off. A shadow flicked over them.

He glanced up.

Kandar, reading the burning words on the page, found his own head held as if in a vise. He wanted to glance up, too; but something held him; the spell of the words chained his eyes to the page. On virgins' skins, flayed and prepared, cured and whitened, fair and clear, ready for the reception of mind-blasting concepts, the book's message hypnotized him. He read on.

Quantoch stirred his legs, stiff from their cramped position. Kandar held him down with one firm hand on his shoulder.

"Do not move, Quantoch. They will think us merely more of the dead."

"No," quavered Quantoch. "No!"

The meanings of Kholokova and Sassilinja branded themselves on Kandar's brain, together with the nauseating means of retaining the spirit of a man slain in battle. He reached the end of the double-spread page. He felt a physical wrench; lights spun before his eyes.

Then he was free from that weird mesmeric power and could look up.

Could look up to the death that descended on them from the sky.

Instinctively his right hand dropped to his left side—but he was wearing no scabbard . . . And Skullskelper had been in the chariot consumed by the green balefire . . .

Unarmed, he could not stand and fight.

"Up!" he shouted at Quantoch. "Swiftly, now!"

The old man tottered erect, all that commanding pose of a scant hour or so ago gone. His face showed the drawn, trembling acceptance of defeat.

Kandar grasped his arm and began to run.

The metal flying ship lazed over them. Ladders depended from her sides, ladders loaded with wolflings like ripe blackberries on loaded dangling branches.

Gasping with the effort, the old man skipped along at Kandar's side, the young prince's strong grip on his arm alone keeping him up and moving. His legs bent and sagged with the strain.

The metal flying ship, like that other that had drifted away from the battle, had been damaged by a flung stone. She answered to the helm slowly. Clumsily she turned to drive over the fleeing Akkarians.

There was a single chance.

The quadriga that had brought Quantoch and his twin brother and Elthalee and Kandar here stood not too far off. The four horses stood patiently, awaiting their next command. If the flying ship was as badly damaged as Kandar hoped, they might be able to outrun the lethal metal flier.

A javelin thudded into the ground beside them.

Kandar lengthened his stride, leaped aboard the chariot and dragged Quantoch bodily after him. He snatched the becketted whip and lashed frenziedly at the horses, all feeling for horse-handling deadened under the frantic urgency of the moment.

A second javelin plunked wickedly into the woodwork.

The horses plunged and reared. They shot off as though demented, their tails and manes blowing wildly. The chariot lurched and bucked after them. Its wheels hissed through the grass. Quantoch clung on, moaning.

The flying ship was turning, turning, swinging around to point its curved prow after them.

Dragging on the reins, Kandar pulled the maddened horses around in a smoking half-circle and cut away at right angles to the ship. He heard the vicious howl go up as the wolflings saw their prey disappearing.

"Hurry, Kandar, hurry!" screamed Quantoch. He was gripping the side rail of the quadriga, rigid, staring after him, a fresh shock dragging him out of that moaning state of near insensibility.

Kandar cast a swift, agonized glance back.

"By Dangorn!" he swore blasphemously.

The wolflings were lowering horses from the ship. Four beasts with broad canvas belts around them, so that their heads and legs dangled down, they swiftly touched the ground. Wolflings jumped from the ladders. In seconds they were pounding after the chariot.

Their weapons gleamed in the static scarlet fire from the sleeping city.

Again and again Kandar lashed the horses. Their sleek backs humped and stretched, humped and stretched. The quadriga bounded over the Plain of Steeds. The wheels hissed through the grass. And behind them the four wolflings clinging like monkeys to the backs of their mounts pounded on, closing the gap, drawing nearer with every lunging stride.

"The shield!" yelled Kandar. "Put up a shield! They'll hurl javelins next!"

Fumbling, trembling, Quantoch unstrapped the smaller of the chariot shields and thrust it up to guard their backs. Almost at once a javelin smacked into it with a nasty thud that told of powerful wolfman muscles at full stretch. Quantoch yelped in surprise.

Ahead lay the wide expanse of the Plain of Steeds. If the horses were left to run, providing they kept a straight line, they could run for miles. Kandar swept another quick glance back. The horses were very near. Jouncing on the flying chariot boards, he quickly knotted the reins loosely to the rail and gave a final savage flailing burst of whip strokes. The horses responded. Foam flew back like breaking wavecrests.

Kandar judged the distances nicely. He drew back his arm. Another javelin thunked against the shield, and Quantoch, crouched down behind it with his whole body braced, yelped.

The whip flashed like a striking snake.

The leading half-man thought he could deal with it.

He grasped the stinging thong and began to pull.

Kandar jammed the butt end of the whip down against the rail of the chariot and hauled back, as though playing a monstrous fish.

The wolfman catapulted from the horse's back, his brass-studded black armor catching the red light and gleaming as though with blood. He let go of the whip as he hit the ground on his face. He smeared himself along the ground, and his horse, without time to avoid him, trampled him into the earth and staggered, collapsing, a dozen yards.

The remaining three galloped on, screeching.

The leading wolfling hurled a javelin. It missed Quantoch's shield, clattered into the well of the chariot and stuck quivering into the wood of the frontboard.

"This can't go on!" screamed Quantoch, not daring to look over the shield rim.

Kandar hadn't liked the nearness of that javelin cast.

He coiled the whip in, flicked it ready for the next lash.

"If they get too close they'll jump us!" He knew enough of the wolfling's purpose to know that. "I wanted to keep the javelin as a last resort, but—"

He dragged the javelin head out from the wood with one explosive burst of savage anger. He poised it, aimed, cast in a blurring of liquid action.

The wolfman's screech was abruptly sliced off as the javelin head sheared through his throat. He toppled from his horse, which raced blindly on.

"Two down, two to go!" panted Kandar.

The other two suddenly became wild with that fierce unconsidering savagery that overwhelms the fighting man balked of his prey. They closed in fast. Their swords lifted.

Through the clatter and bang of chariot and horses, the stiffly snorting breath of the animals, the whirring hiss of the tall wheels through grass, Kandar could plainly hear the obscene screeching of the wolfmen. He looped the lash delicately.

He snapped the thong out in a vicious cutting slash.

The right-hand wolfling took the lash about his neck. It coiled. Kandar hauled back. The wolfman clung on. The chariot and the horses thundered now alongside.

Any minute now . . . Kandar ducked his head and glanced back. The left-hand wolfling was leaning out from his mount's back, the sword leaping in his gray hand, his muzzled face savage with unholy venom.

"Quantoch!" yelled Kandar.

He dragged the whip handle one last time, then turned and lunged across the chariot.

The wolfling's sword swept down.

Quivering, quaking, querulous, Quantoch screamed and fell back. The action saved his life.

The sword slashed down in a long raking diagonal arc across the *Thaumalogicon*. Parchment of virgins' skin ripped. Dragonskin binding sundered. A great diagonal wedge of the book ripped away and fell overside to be lost in the pounding, writhing dust of their passage.

But the tip of the sword, protruding beyond the thickness of the book, leaped back reddened. Crimson with the blood of the necromancer Quantoch, the sword lifted high for another slash that this time would be final.

The chariot shield edge felt thick and rimmed bronze beneath Kandar's clutching fingers. He dragged the heart-shaped shield up from Quantoch's nerveless hands and swung it, like a great murderous discus. He felt the downward blow of the sword gong on the shield. Then the edge buzz-sawed into the wolfling's throat above the collar of his black and brass armor.

The wolfling's scream of triumph changed to a choked glottal stop of agony.

Without checking his movement Kandar swung the shield skimmingly around from left to right. He made it only just in time. The right-hand wolfman's sword in turn clanged down on the shield. This time the edge took him across the face.

Black-gummed muzzle and yellow teeth smashed back in crushed ruin. Red blood gushed. Nauseated, Kandar flung the shield into the well of the chariot. The two wolflings' horses galloped off, their backs bare.

He bent beside Quantoch.

The old eyes regarded him with a sunken light. The wizened cheeks showed shriveled like dried fruit skins.

"Kandar . . . my prince . . . you must . . . " Quantoch could not go on. He swallowed weakly and his eyelids closed.

Kandar saw at once that the wound had been deep and severe, slicing down the old man's side where the blood dappled the gorgeous green and gold robes. He knew what Quantoch meant. He looked intently, his eyes narrowing against the afternoon glare, searching the sky.

The wolfling's metal ship was drifting aimlessly,

pushed by the little breeze away from the city. There seemed little more danger to fear from her. The chariot horses ran on, blowing, plunging, carrying them away from the city. Kandar rose and unknotted the reins, swung the quadriga around in a slewing half-circle, raising dust, sent the horses pounding back toward the ensorcelled city of Lost Ferranoz.

Weakly, Quantoch's voice reached him: "You must—look for—help—from yourself." A long pause as the quadriga leaped towards the silent city. Then: "You yourself—my prince—only you—left." Kandar did not look down. "You should—have—studied—" came the fluttering whisper. "Now—the necessary enchantments—you must—*must*—seek a greater power than the evil intelligences!" His voice gushed with a spurious strength, stronger, fey.

"A power stronger than my power, a knowledge that can overcome the stasis drowning Dreaming Ferranoz!"

"Yes, Quantoch, yes," said Kandar, and he lashed the horses again.

"The book—" Again Quantoch's quavering voice sounded. Kandar heard labored, muffled movement. Still he did not look down. "I have unlocked . . . chains . . ." Quantoch's voice dribbled away.

At a passionate headlong pace Kandar brought the quadriga to the gate of Ferranoz that led onto the Imperial Way. Inside that gate among the inferno and the battle, forms showed sinewy in arrested strength, unmoving, statuesque. Kandar slammed the chariot to a halt without a glance for the macabre desolation within the gate. The Imperial Way, he had seen that before. What was being non-enacted there right now could no longer arouse in him glance for the macabre desolation within the gate. The Imperial Way, he had seen that before. What was being non-emotions of horror. He grasped Quantoch gently, eased him off the chariot tail onto his broad shoulders, ran with him toward the gate.

The Gate of Happy Returns.

That was the name of this gate that led onto the Imperial Way.

The savage irony of that name in these circumstances wounded Kandar as he ran. He could see where Quarmeln, carrying Elthalee, had collapsed just within the magic aura of the enchantment binding Ferranoz. Carefully, he laid Quantoch down and pushed him, gently, through the gateway. The gorgeous blood-dappled green and gold robes rucked on rutted marble. The necromancer's tall conical cap had been lost, it seemed, eons ago.

With a last final careful nudge Kandar pushed Quantoch's foot. He felt a strange gnawing, biting, quivering tingling in his fingers and, frightened to sickness, snatched his hand away. That eerie tingling in his fingers had been the first symptom of the spell that had engulfed the city. He sweated, suddenly cold with fear.

Hardly comprehending why, he was reminded of the wheel and Maggra's oiled body turning the handle and the fluttering lacy blue and green sparks. That had happened in the retreat he kept a secret from all but a few intimates. That had happened this morning.

An age ago.

He walked back to the mutilated copy of the *Thaumalogicon,* sat down, and after a careful scrutiny of his surroundings in search of wolflings, began to read.

He felt the power and force of what he read. He felt the dynamism so much more powerful than the feeble blue sparks he had culled from his wheel. Quantoch wielded a greater power than ever science could hope for, but . . . but a rebellious spirit still struggled in Kandar's mind; he still stubbornly clung to his belief in his eventual power and majesty of science.

But now he squatted in the dirt outside an ensorcelled city's walls and read profane lore from arcane minds, written down on the fair skins of virgins. He tried to remember what he read. The words were difficult. The memory could hold them easily enough by rote; but to juggle an entire concept in the mind long enough for the spell to take, there—there was the magic and the mystery.

Many of the spells lacked beginnings or ends, the sundered portions lost in a billowing paper chase across the Plain of Steeds.

At last, as the sun began a faster slide towards the western ocean, he knew he had read all there was to read and had committed to his memory all his mind could hold. Now he must be about his business in life.

He hefted the *Thaumalogicon* in his hands.

Whatever was to happen to him in the future, he knew that many passages to come would not be pleasant; he knew his life would be hard and rugged. He could not possibly carry a heavy tome like this around with him everywhere he went. He riffled the pages reflectively, hearing them rustle, hearing their sussuration with all its ominous meanings gone for him. He had read the book, had he not? That experience had changed him, as much else this day had changed him.

With a single heave he tossed the book into the Gate of Happy Returns. It hit the marble, bounced in a fluff of pages, like a girl in billowing skirts curtseying, and then lay still and silent beside the still and silent form of Quantoch.

He went toward the quadriga, conscious of his hunger and thirst, seeing in the encroaching shadows a chance to feed and water his horses and to find food for himself. But before the last of the light went, he looked steadily toward the north.

"Thurdur the Cunning," he breathed softly. "You and I, Thurdur the Cunning, have need of words."

Chapter Three

Wherein one of six slighted Kandar's honor and how a whisper became a shout.

Kandar of Ferranoz rode a foundering horse to death over the high shoulder of the Langaan Hills. He rode fast and hard, mercilessly, for death rode at his heels. Around him beneath a brazen sky as cruel as an Emperor's torture chamber stretched a tumbled wilderness of fractured

37

rocks. His lips, cracked and black, were stretched in a mirthless grin. Ever and anon he turned painfully in the saddle to stare with heat-seared eyes back along the burning track.

He had drunk no water for two days, and his throat and mouth, his whole body, screamed silently against the parching dryness.

Fragments of ideas, mutilated concepts, floated around the aching vacuum of his brain. He kept trying wearily to pin down a spell entire, to hold one of the gyrating enchantments long enough to hurl the sorcery at the pursuers riding like the hounds of Death behind him.

Where they had come from, who they were, he had no idea. He had fallen in with a small caravan laden with the furs of the south that fetched high prices in the northern lands where along the uplands the heat was tempered too keenly by altitude. That caravan and all its furs, its gold and its women had been gulped up by the brigands of these yellow hills.

Alone, friendless, with a foundering horse and a cheap bazaar blade at his side, Prince Kandar of Ferranoz rode for his life. Much had happened to him since he had set out from Doomed Akkar; much that had changed him, hardened him, tempered him, further disguised his enormous strength within a lean and sinewy frame that seemed at first sight to be frail and underfed.

Echoing from the crags, a triumphant view-halloo clamored down the track. Stiffly, he turned to look back. Bald, painted heads, bent low over horses' manes, and the shimmer of bright weapons told him that unless he could exert one last effort, his hour had come.

His horse lolloped around the high curve of the trail over the shoulder of the Langaan Hills, and there, opening out below him like a vision from Helios, lay a broad expanse of verdant grassland, with clumped woods and winding smiling streams and—greatest joy—tucked demurely into the curve of the river stood a city, a proud, shining, towered city.

Kandar kicked his horse's flanks. If he could keep ahead of the pursuit until he reached the plains, there should be men there who would hold a traditional grudge fight against these wolves of the mountains. He rephrased that in his tired mind; not wolves; these were men. He had left the wolflings long ago.

His horse, tired and spent, stumbled on a loose stone.

Wearily, slowly, not yet responding to the final moment of crisis, Kandar grabbed for the saddle bow.

The horse's legs slid from under him, and in a smother of dust and small stones he went down.

The final acceptance of the accident sent a rush of blood coursing through Kandar. If he was to die, then he'd die well and proudly, and he'd take as many of these painted, bald-headed bandits with him as he could.

The bazaar sword felt ill at ease in his hand, used as he was to master armorer's work in the true blade Skullskelper, but he hefted it and fell into a posture of defense.

There were six of them.

Outriders of the band that had destroyed the fur caravan, they had hunted him through the barren hills more for the sport of it, more to satiate their blood lust, than for the looting of his dead body.

The sun beat down. Dust lay thickly on the stones. The trail to safety stretched behind him, down the slope to the plains. But the first step on that, the moment he turned his back, he would be done for, finished.

They rushed him, low on their horses' necks, seeking to overpower him at a stroke for their subsequent pleasure.

He threw himself sideways and snatched at two of the lances driving in toward him. Caught up, as though on the parallel bars of the recreation rooms back in Dreaming Ferranoz, he was carried along for a dozen steps. Then he broke one lance and using the point with savage force drove it harshly through the robed body of the nearest bandit. The man whooshed his surprise.

The second bandit felt the bite of the bazaar sword. It gnawed deeply into the side of his neck. Kandar wrenched it free. The blade snappped, about a third of the way along from the hilt, where a fancy trade name had been etched. With a furious yell Kandar hurled the stump of sword into the face of the third bandit, striving to spear him over the body of his companion.

The other three, bunched out in that initial charge,

reined in, swung their horses, panting and scrabbling on the rocks, rising on their rear hooves, swung them around for another pass.

Kandar glanced up with a long look of savage hatred.

He had no quarrel with these hill bandits—then they rushed again. This time he was able to meet their lance thrust with a snatched-up spear, to pike one man off and stab him in the throat, hard, so that the spearhead ground on rock, before turning to dodge a spear thrust and to grab that spear, pull, and to dispatch that one.

The last one hauled in his steed and turned. He sat his horse for a long moment, eyeing Kandar. Kandar, panting, hefted a new spear.

"What are you waiting for?" he taunted. He gestured about him. Five dead men lay in the broiling sun. "Come and join your friends!"

The man lifted in the stirrups. Then he slumped back and turned to ride away. Evidently, he thought better of attacking this single solitary traveller without help. Now, he thought that . . .

Wild fury coruscated through Kandar. He took the insult of this, the injustice, very personally.

"No!" he shouted, high and hard, dominatingly. "No, by Dangorn, no!"

Hefting the spear, he poised, threw, sent the shaft to bury eight inches of its steel head in the back of the departing bandit. The man jerked upright, shocked, his backbone sheared clean through. Then, like a hop pocket, he tumbled out of the saddle.

Kandar walked up to stand over him.

"No miserable mortal insults the son of the God-Emperor Heliodotus with impunity!"

He walked away without touching the body.

His mouth was flooded with saliva.

He found the water bottles belonging to the dead men and collected them into a bunch, hanging by their leathern straps. He rounded up four of the horses. Two had galloped off, and his own had to be killed neatly, having broken a leg in his fall.

Kandar hated this. He raged at the stupidity of whatever nature it was that allowed so beautiful a creature as a horse no chance of life once its leg was broken.

40

Soon, having eaten and drunk sparingly, he was in the saddle once again and leading three bridle horses. Thoughtfully, he picked up all the arms scattered about and selected the best sword, a partially curved blade of a make unknown to him, but with the ring of finely tempered iron. The hilt fitted his hand well enough. It would do; not having Skullskelper, it would have to do.

He rode down the sun-scorched track and out onto the plain. He rode toward the city in its curve of river.

The city struck Kandar as strange. No one bothered to challenge him as he entered the gateways, although soldiers in steel caps lounged on guard. Many people in white robes and colored shawls scurried about their business, and the sound of bartering filled the lazy air. The streets were narrow and packed close together because the houses were so small. Mere white adobe shells, they could not have been more than a two- or three-room size, a mere fleabite to the sizes of even the smaller houses of Ferranoz.

Kandar rode slowly, searching for an inn. Finally he spotted a hard and tarnished leather bottle hanging from a beam over a door and turned his horses' heads that way.

The tavern was just the same as many others Kandar had sampled on his way north and yet . . . and yet . . . there was this strange difference he had sensed about the city. He put this feeling of strangeness down to the many different races and nationalities and colors of men and women here. Evidently, this city stood at a crossroads—the road through the mountains met the parallel road, and here they crossed the river. No wonder many caravans met here.

This city of Gilgal must act as the entrepôt for the whole area from the mountains right across to the Sea of Dreams. As the coastline had tended ever more and more westerly, Kandar had left the seashore to strike more directly north. Now, he could ask the usual questions.

The tavern boasted a long bar running all down one side of the low-ceilinged room behind which, Kandar guessed, would be situated the living quarters for the innkeeper and his family and retainers. The center of the room had been left empty, swept and sanded, tables and chairs and benches ranged about the central open space.

Here, Kandar surmised with an amused casual chuckle, the dancing girls would soon prance out to go through their routine of throwing brightly colored veils hither and yon.

"By Ganchi! I'm tired!" he said to himself. But he could not sleep this night until he had asked his question.

After a number of tavern brawls he had discovered that it paid not to be too brash about it. He arranged for a room for the night, and stabling for the horses, and then cuddled a wine goblet in a shadowy corner. Presently, as was inevitable in a certain class of establishment, a girl wafted out of the candlelight toward him. She showed an expanse of bosom and thigh, between which a red velvet costume showed wrinkle marks and stains that a dinner hurriedly eaten might leave.

"Hullo, soldier boy," she said with a smile.

Kandar did not disabuse her. He wore a simple blue tunic, and trousers tucked into mid-thigh leather snake-boots. The brown well-worn leather belt with the slings for a scabbard was the only item of clothing or equipment he had retained from Lost Ferranoz. He shifted the bandit's scabbard so that the girl could sit beside him. He poured her wine. She had brought her own goblet.

Her face consisted of a red mouth, a stub nose, a pair of brown eyes, surrounded by a mop of frizzed blonde hair. She looked tired, anxious to please, and thankful to sit down.

"I'm Aylee," she opened the conversation.

"That's nice," said Kandar, replenishing her glass.

She summed up this lean rangy man as a moody one, a man who didn't like the sound of his own voice. Every man, in Aylee's experience, had a guilty past. This one, now, he'd probably murdered his employer and raped his daughter and then run away and joined a band of mercenaries. Well. That kind made good tavern fodder.

Their table stood at an angle to another around which lolled four lean tavern wolves—again Kandar winced inwardly at that hated simile, for these were men, not wolflings—who drank and diced casually, by their talk waiting for a fifth to join them. They wore leather buskins and tunics, loose, easy-fitting garments suitable to men who hunted. Each man's sword, high-slung across his back, was a long and thin rapier of a style unfamiliar to Kandar. On the table four broad-brimmed hats trimmed with exotic bird feathers added a splash of color beneath the candles.

Kandar's casual conversation with Aylee meandered on. He wanted her primed and ripe when he asked her the question.

He had summed her up. At one time he would have felt a priggish distaste; now, as one unfortunate to another, he would regard her as a sister in misfortune. At last, he thought, he could open the subject of conversation that burned in him. He could not, in very truth, have remained silent about that much longer.

"Tell me," he said, refilling her goblet as he spoke, "Aylee, what you know of Thurdur the Cunning."

He might have tossed an opened basket of black vipers into the tavern.

As one, men and women rose from their benches and chairs; like a rippled wave they reeled back from him. He had not realized how loudly he had spoken—he had not spoken loudly—he had been whispering!

Then how came all these people to have heard him so clearly? How did they recoil from a whisper that had trumpeted throughout the tavern?

"Thurdur the Cunning!"

His whisper had magnified into a mighty shout!

He, too, started up, and his right hand reached across to grasp the hilt of the bandit sword.

"Swords will not help you now!" gasped Aylee. She clawed back, on her knees, her hands clutched tightly together and pressed against her red-velvet-covered breasts. Her face looked ghastly. All their faces looked ghastly.

A wavering shimmer, as of light at the end of a long dark tunnel, began in the center of the tavern. Like a spectral image, glowing with baleful fires, it grew and swelled, bloating from a spot to a line to an expanding form that towered up in gigantic lineaments that solidified into the awesome glowing shape of . . . of . . .

Kandar had no words for the apparition.

He could make out dimly in the blazing illumination pouring from the thing a horned head, flowing robes, the hint of steel mesh, and from the specter radiated a dark force of absolute power over all those present.

Gasps and prayers to Bright Gyrane spattered like wind-blown raindrops from the cowed men and women. Kandar felt his skin go cold. A slick sweat gathered on him.

He forced his legs to hold him up. With his hand uselessly fixed to the sword hilt he stared at the weird form.

A voice whispered like a scalpel.

"Some one called on Thurdur the Cunning. I am come to find that one and take him to my master!"

Recklessly, Kandar shouted back.

"I am Prince Kandar of Ferranoz, son of Pandin Heliodotus, God-Emperor of all Akkar! I call on Thurdur the Cunning, for I need his help!"

A tiny scrap of knowledge bubbled up in his mind, a spell committed to memory by rote and now almost fully formed in his mind. He caught and grasped at it, unformed, incomplete, there in his own brain. Once again he saw the blasphemous words written on skins of virgins. The words danced before his mind's eye.

"On the conjuring of the Caul of Preservation against those who—" but the rest would not come. Numbly, he spoke the words he remembered.

The fires of the phantom form flickered more brightly.

The scalpel voice keened again. "A wight who bandies petty spells! A mortal who dares to call on forces beyond his comprehension!"

A whirlwind blew gustily about that frightful form. Lights span. The sand strewing the floor of the tavern whirled into a willy-willy. Kandar felt the hair of his head lifting in that ghostly breeze.

The people of the tavern moaned.

A long pointing arm of fire gestured imperiously.

"You wished to see my master! I, his minion Myder, am come to bring you to him!"

A bench stood close by Kandar. A simple wooden bench of dark oak split and curved, grease-dark with ages of spilled meals and hasty wipings, it stood on four stubby legs. A force against which Kandar had no defense pushed him. It was like a pillow thrust against his chest.

Awkwardly he sprawled back, sat on the bench. He straddled it.

The bench moved! It stirred! It lifted into the air!

Gripping with numbed hands, Kandar was lifted on the bench. As though riding a ghostly steed of midnight he was carried across the floor. Men and women stumbled and fell and jostled to clear a path for him.

The door crashed open. Starlight glittered down. The bench increased its speed. As though galloping a blasphemous mount from the nether pits, Kandar hurled from the door. The flaming form of Myder followed. Night wind tore at Kandar's clothes, his hair. He bent his head. Headlong through the night the bench flew. Shepherded by Myder, the bench carried him helplessly toward his sought-for meeting with Thurdur the Cunning.

Chapter Four

Of the demand of Thurdur the Cunning and how Krak the Mighty sought to slay phantoms of the mind.

Over the rooftops of proud Gilgal flew the bench. The towers and the close-packed small houses passed beneath. As though in a nightmare Kandar was carried willy-nilly through the night air.

Straight toward the tallest of the towers he lunged. Tall, many-turreted, battlemented, built of a black stone that seemed to engulf light, the tower raised a blasphemous finger of scorn. Lights twinkled from many windows, lights that struggled, it seemed, to cast their glow outwards from the ebony pile.

"The Tower of Taractacus, King of Taractea, Overlord of all the lands from the Langaan Hills to the sea" came

Myder's voice, like a knife blade against the booming of the wind. "Yonder lives my master, Thurdur the Cunning."

They hurtled windswept toward a lightless tower jutting from the side of the main mass, a tower from which a breath of doom seemed to reach out to grasp Kandar with the stench of decay.

The bench shot into an arched opening and then, making Kandar's flesh crawl, it ran along on its four stumpy wooden legs, clicking and clattering on flagstones. By the effulgence of Myder's radiation Kandar saw before him a chamber spanning the width of the side tower, a chamber furnished in a way that made him catch his breath.

Quantoch on the Plain of Steeds outside burning beautiful Lost Ferranoz had said, "Thurdur the Cunning has a power in his own land commensurate with mine—"

Yet this sorcerer's chamber showed at a glance a cabalistic refinement, a luxury, a decadence, that the court necromancer of Dreaming Ferranoz would have despised and abhorred.

Flung from the bench, Kandar sprawled on rugs he recognized as brought from Sanghara. A pang of remembrance shot through him. By Myder's light the weird and obscene artifacts in the chamber glared back, lit and shadowed, seeming to move, repugnant, horrid. Kandar lay where he had fallen, breathing deeply, waiting for the owner of this necromantic hell to appear.

When Thurdur the Cunning appeared, he walked slowly in through an iron-bound doorway. Kandar felt a sickly sense of tension increased rather than diminished by that simple entrance; expecting fire and brimstone, coruscating apparitions, the reality made him realize the awfulness of what might still happen. Yet he stood up, straight and tall and strong, lean-faced and determined. For this, he had traveled far.

"So this is the half-witted loon who calls on Thurdur the Cunning! This is the starveling prince who bandies petty spells!"

The wizard wore a long cabalistically inscribed gown with runes of repute running hypnotically along the hems, similar to that worn by Quantoch; but instead of a tall conical cap he wore a bright red hat with broad brim and

46

low, square-sided crown. Stars and half-moons embroidered in diamonds and rubies and emeralds splashed bright color from his person; he glittered in the light of Myder.

"I have come far—" began Kandar.

"You have come from Akkar, from Doomed Ferranoz! I know! I know!"

Kandar could not take his eyes from the great dragon-skin-bound tome fastened to Thurdur's waist by golden chains. Of a deep smoky yellow color, the skin showed clearly why this volume was called *The Ochre Scroll.*

Thurdur touched the book with one veined hand. Old, he looked, old with years of evil incantations bearing down his spirit. Debauchery and dissipation showed in his face, in the watery bags beneath his faded eyes, in the parchment skin, sagging beneath his chin. He opened a thin mouth with blackened lips and gums to reveal snaggled yellow teeth, some missing, and a brown tongue that rasped unpleasantly against that withered mouth.

"Quantoch I know. An old fool! A dodderer! A man unfit to be called a necromancer!"

"Quantoch," said Kandar firmly, "is sore wounded unto death. I have come to—"

"Ferranoz burns!" chuckled Thurdur the Cunning. His thin body moved in an ungainly dance beneath the heavy robe. "Now King Taractacus must invade all the fair land of Akkar and claim it for his own!" A fierce dominance burned evilly in Thurdur the Cunning. "For years I have counseled him to attack, and for years he has resisted my advice. But now—now he must listen!"

Kandar laughed.

Some of his daunted spirit surged up afresh.

"You are deluded!" he said, harshly, forcing himself to remember that he was a son of the God-Emperor, Pandin Heliodotus. "Of what use to you—to anyone—now, is Dreaming Ferranoz?"

"What mean you, boy?" Thurdur bent forward, like a snake, his faded eyes flaring with a baffled wrath. "Speak, before I blast you where you stand!"

"You, the great sorcerer—and you do not know what has befallen my dear city of Ferranoz!"

Angrily, Thurdur raised his right hand, the long bony

47

fingers clawed. The maddening light from Myder wavered and sent long shadows crawling.

"Listen, Thurdur the Cunning!" snapped Kandar. "A great doom fell on my city and my land." Quickly he related what had happened. "Now, I need the knowledge contained in *The Ochre Scroll,* to learn how Ferranoz can be saved from the devilish ensorcellment."

Thurdur paused. He considered, his bony chin cupped in bony hand. His face showed all the malevolent cunning for which he had been named.

"The king would not thank me to advise him to conquer an ensorcelled land," he said, thoughtfully, his faded eyes fixed on Kandar. "Of what use a city transfixed by a spell?" His hand touched the tome chained to his waist. "But you spoke of greater powers?"

Kandar nodded. "The way will be shown to me. I am sure of that. *The Trilogos Damnae—*"

At the words Thurdur drew himself up, his face working. A light of madness flared in his eyes, Myder's light caught and reflected in those evil orbs. He stretched out a hand, a long and skinny finger pointed at Kandar.

"Boy! Be careful! You do not know with what powers of darkness you so lightly play!"

Kandar again felt that ghostly crawl of fear breeze through him.

"Listen, Kandar of Ferranoz, Lion of Akkar—will you sell your soul to save your city and your land and your people?"

long and weary road for this moment of time. Now he

Kandar knew in that instant that a great moment of his life had arrived. He stood at a crossroads. He had come a must face, squarely, just how much of himself he would give to rescue his father and Elthalee, to save Quantoch and Quarmeln, to succour Sheldion.

He did not make the decision without thought. Agonisedly, he tried to thrust away the decision. But he knew he could not. He was a prince of Akkar, a son of the God-Emperor. His duty lay clearly before him; his duty and his love compelled him. There was no other course than the one he saw before him.

"Yes," he said firmly. "Anything that is needed to be

done to save Dreaming Ferranoz, that I will do."

"Ah!"

Myder's light wove a net of shifting colors within the sorcerer's chamber. A chuckling, whistling, evil laugh broke from that demoniac figure.

"This is what you must do." Thurdur the Cunning had taken up at once the chance offered him; he knew, Kandar could see with a tremor of intent, exactly what he was about. "You must do a small task for me, a trifle, and then I will reveal to you what secrets you require from *The Ochre Scroll*."

"A task?"

"Outside the city walls—outside, for he dare not enter here!—dwells a miserable being called Tosho. Tosho of the small talents. Him you will kill and take from his body the small jade casket he forever keeps next to his heart."

"Why should I kill him? I do not know him. He has done me no harm."

"Fool! You require something of me. This is the price you must pay!"

"And my soul?"

"When you bring me the jade casket and tell me Tosho is dead, then, only then, Akkarian, can we discuss your future."

Any compunction for this unknown man called Tosho of the small talents could not weigh for an instant in Kandar's mental balance against his concern for his city and his people. Anything he had to do he would do, he had said. Somberly, he knew that to be true, however unpalatable it might be.

He nodded.

"Very well, Thurdur the Cunning. I will kill Tosho of the small talents and take from him the casket of jade."

"Begone, then!" Thurdur moved his fingers in a cryptic gesture.

Once more the wooden bench flew with Kandar seated astride, out and away over the huddled rooftops of sleeping Gilgal. Out and away, over the wall where sleepy guards did not bother to look up—did not bother or, more probably, did not dare. For Kandar had recognized the reason for that strangeness in this city, this city that, with King

Taractacus as its titular head, was yet ruled by arcane arts by Thurdur the Cunning.

The countryside lay dark and asleep all about. With only a rush of wind in his hair and clothes to break the silence Kandar hurtled on. Open fields passed below. Then came trees, clumping, growing ever more closely together, until at last he flew low over a wide forest where the trees formed a vast canopy shutting out all sight of the ground beneath.

The bench angled down. Controlled by Thurdur from his ebony tower, the bench slowed, sought an opening in the trees, and thumped down to bump against a mossy bank. At once, seeming never to have been capable of levitation, it became only an oaken bench.

Kandar dismounted.

He had been given no directions. But he knew well enough that from now on in his quest he must forge on and find directions for himself. He began to walk toward a trail that debouched into the clearing. He did not bother to look back at the bench. If it was still there when he returned with the jade casket, all well and good. If not, then he would walk back to Gilgal.

Whatever happened, he promised himself, he would carry out Thurdur's charge. He had it in mind to ask that man of evil lore many questions, questions that might help him solve the mystery of the intelligences who had hurled the gray wolfling horde against Fair Ferranoz. He walked through the forest carefully, the bandit sword loose in its scabbard, his senses alert.

Very soon he came to an upthrust mass of rock lifting from the forest floor, where three trails converged and where the trees grew into an overhanging bower. The dark shape of a cave mouth beckoned in the face of the rock. Half obscured by trailing fronds and vines, the dark hole promised unknown dangers.

The pervading gloom could not hold Kandar back.

Boldly he advanced on the cave. Here, obviously, was where Tosho of the small talents dwelled.

A looping wash of scarlet funley-flowers grew all alongside the cave mouth. Kandar, seeing their color brighten as he advanced, halted in surprise. Only then the source of the light became apparent; a line of resinous torches burned and sputtered, debouching from the left-hand forest trail. Each torch was carried in the left hand of a gigantic brown-skinned warrior. Each muscular right hand grasped a giant broadsword. A sword and a torch in hand, the warriors raced silently over the dead leaves of the trail.

Then, leaping, cutting, slashing, an enormous figure burst into view.

Kandar halted, and his grip on his sword tightened.

The white-skinned giant—he must have been at least seven feet tall—with wildly blowing yellow hair and glittering blue eyes, fought with an incredible savage fury against the running dark-skinned warriors. Clad in a tigerskin loincloth, naked of foot, his body a white dynamo of destruction, the huge barbarian hacked and slashed and thrust—yet the warriors raced past him unheeding and unhurt.

Clearly, Kandar saw one tremendous slash of the sword pass clean through the middle of a warrior. Yet the man did not fall!

Running at the white barbarian's heels, the slender white form of a girl flitted uncannily through the torch-light. Her long red hair swirled as she ran. Fleet of foot she was, lithe, beautifully formed with firm breasts and long thighs, yet she had to run at top speed to keep pace with the enormous bounds of the giant and the silent pantherish tread of the dark warriors.

"What deviltry have I run into now?" asked Kandar as he pressed back against the rock, alongside the cave mouth, half-hidden by the profusion of the funley-flowers. He did not think that Thurdur's cunning had envisaged this.

Now a clearer pattern emerged. The dark warriors had been trying to keep the giant back. With demoniac yells of barbaric fury he had flung himself against that seemingly steel-strong line of fighting men—only to feel his sword cut through empty air. Now he charged like a maddened bull in the arena smashing down the barricades.

"Come out, you quaking curs!" roared the giant.

His voice boomed and rolled against the rock, echoing back like a clashing roll of thunder.

Lit by that lurid unearthly light carried by the spectral
51

warriors, the scene before the cave mouth jumbled into a crazed madness. Kandar understood that enchantments had brought the insubstantial warriors into ephemeral being, and he guessed that this was the handiwork of Tosho of the small talents.

Not so small! The warriors would have cowed a lesser mortal than the blond giant who now ran berserker-like toward the cave mouth.

The girl, her hair aflame in the torches' lights, followed him. Her face, the eyes wide with the enormity of the moment, saw Kandar, half-hidden among the funley-flowers.

At once she called out, high and frightened.

"Krak! Here is one for your blade!"

The barbarian swerved in his dead run. He saw Kandar. His great sword lifted high, glittering in the lurid glare.

"I see you, little man! Now you will taste the steel of Krak the Mighty!"

At that moment a movement shuffled stealthily in the entrance to the cave. Momentarily, Kandar saw the man who cowered there, a small man, withered, dry like a twig, wearing a tattered robe spangled with the stars and crescent moons of a warlock.

Tosho—it must be, Tosho of the small talents.

His face looked that of a monkey of the eastern lands of Remisthet. Hooked nose, full mouth, a fuzz of white hair at sides and beneath his chin, his face peered out blindly. Over his eyes were two pieces of glass, hanging in a wire frame, strange goggling double-eyes Kandar found frightening and funny, at the same time.

"They have come!" Tosho squeaked, like a rabbit whose neck is bitten through by a terrier. "My arts are small, small, I do not have the powers—"

Despite the nearness of the giant, Krak the Mighty, who would be on him in a half dozen strides, Kandar still stared at the shrinking figure of Tosho. Was there a bulge beneath that robe, a hump over the heart?

Then there was no more time for coherent thought, no time to dredge a spell from his shaky store and form it into a concept in his mind to hurl at the foaming barbarian. Now there was time only to fling up his own blade and meet the barbarian's steel in a clang of metal.

Chapter Five

How Tosho of the small talents and Krak the Mighty,
being dead, yet lived.

"This one stands!" roared Krak the Mighty joyfully. "This one is no phantom of dreams!"

He swung his great sword in a blur of metal against Kandar. All the arts of swordplay so long and thoroughly learned served the Akkarian now. Never had he been matched against so ferocious, so completely dominating, a swordsman as this before. Many long hours spent sweating in the sun of far Akkar pitted against the best the Empire could bring had honed and sharpened his swordmanship to a point where he had yet to acknowledge a master. Yet here he was up against not only skill in handling a sword, but so much power-packed muscle, so much sheer savage weight, that he was battered back almost at a run away from the funley-flowers and across the clearing.

Krak the Mighty enjoyed his work. His massively muscled arm rose and fell, his great sword hacked and cut, thrust and stabbed, and all the time his broad, battered face with the startling blue eyes bore a great beam of pure pleasure. Here was a man born for battle.

Kandar saw at once that only speed and skill could save him. Not a single chance in hell existed for him to tire the giant, to wear him down, to beat down his blade for the killing thrust. He must work him around, draw him over to the rock face again, where fallen boulders strewed the ground. Obligingly, obsessed with the battle fury upon him, the blond barbarian followed.

Kandar's arm jarred to the force of the giant's strokes. He felt as though he was holding his blade against an avalanche of steel.

53

Yet he twisted and turned, slipped blows, deflected that murderous brand. He detected Krak's fondness for the edge, his delight in the broad sweeping slash that would make a man's head jump from his shoulders.

He ducked his head and felt the wind of the blow ruffle his hair. Then he leaned in, his lithe body taut like a bowstring, and pinked the giant on his broad chest so that a runnel of bright blood sprang out.

"Ho! So you bite, little one!" roared Krak and brought his blade down swishingly.

Only a frantic backward plunge and a rolling twist of his body saved Kandar from being sliced from crown to shoulderbone.

He tossed his head up and swung his own blade at Krak's waist, halted the blow's direction, and sliced down a thewed thigh. A line of fresh blood showed on Krak's white skin.

"So you claw, as well! You fight like a man!"

There was no question of Kandar's being wounded.

A single touch of that blade wielded by those giant muscles would be the end. His head, an arm, a leg, anything the barbarian's sword struck would be smitten off like a butcher slicing meat.

Now they were back by the cave mouth. Against the blur of steel opposed to him Kandar fought with a passionate devotion to his art.

He felt boulders beneath his feet. In a fragmentary crazily tilted vision he caught a glimpse of Tosho standing by the cave entrance, still, taut, his wizened face a mask of terror. At his side crouched the white nude form of the girl, her brazen hair swaying before her as she peered up at that titanic conflict.

More boulders beneath his feet. He moved carefully, cautiously. A last-minute skip to the side drew Krak on. The barbarian's blade whistled down, and Kandar flung himself sideways. At once Krak checked himself, his incredible musculature hauling back on a blow that would have decapitated his opponent.

Then Krak stepped on a round boulder.

His foot skidded.

The sword flew up in instant reaction.

Almost, almost Kandar did not complete his thrust. A

great joy that possessed Krak the Mighty had communicated itself to him, so that despite the almost insuperable odds and the desperateness of the battle he had enjoyed this fight more than any other. Almost, almost but not quite, he stopped his lunge.

But long training and the knowledge that he battled his own death drove his point long and deeply into the giant's body. Neatly between the ribs the bandit blade slid. Its point skewered the mighty barbarian heart of Krak.

For an instant the giant stood, stupefied, not believing, looking down to where the sword impaled him. Kandar skipped back, leaving the sword in the proudest sheath it would ever know.

"You—" said Krak, in a soft, strange voice. "You are a fine-plucked 'un—little man—"

Then he fell on his face and died.

With a single sweep of action, incensed, driven by his fears, by his own courage, by the demons that goaded him on, Kandar leaped for the fallen giant's sword. He lifted it, feeling its weight, ponderous yet balanced.

A movement scurried behind him.

Tosho of the small talents stood there, hand outstretched, finger pointing at Kandar. Strange words began spatter from the wizard's lips. A horrible numbness began to spatter from the wizard's lips. A horrible numbness began to grip Kandar. With a single bound he leaped forward and in a despairing sweep of the sword swung the blade in a flat arc.

Tosho's head flew from his shoulders to bound gorily among the rocks.

Sobbing with the efforts of a moment past, Kandar leaned on the sword. He panted for breath.

Only he and the naked girl were left alive in the clearing. No sight or sound remained of the phantom dark warriors, and Tosho's headless corpse collapsed at his feet, while Krak's mighty body lolled in death among the boulders.

With an inarticulate cry, a muffled sound of an animal in pain, the girl ran toward Krak's body and dropped beside it. Her red hair, dark and unflaming now the torchlight had gone, draped across the magnificent bared torso. Her breasts crushed against Krak's great rib cage. She

55

turned her head to glare at Kandar. He saw her face, pinched, tight, hating, the eyes black pits of hell.

"I . . ." faltered Kandar. He took a step forward.

Like a fawn of the woodlands the girl leaped up. Her white body flashed like a sliver of moonlight in the clearing. She darted past Kandar. He turned to look after her.

She was bending beside the headless body of Tosho. Long, slender fingers burrowed beneath his star-spangled robe. The girl gave a cry of triumph. Immediate comprehension hit Kandar. He started forward.

"That is mine!" he shouted. "That is what I have come for!"

She glared up at him, panting, her chest heaving unsteadily, her hair swinging wildly as she shook her head. In her hand, just withdrawn from Tosho's robe, lay a small, rectangular jade casket.

"It is mine!" she screamed at him. He found her hard to understand; she spoke the language of Akkar, the language used by everyone on this continent, thickly, with more than the impediment of a mere accent. Krak the Mighty had spoken a crude dialect form but at least that had been his normal tongue. This girl, Kandar knew, had had to learn Akkarian.

Kandar moved Krak's sword point forward. He pressed the tip into the girl's navel.

Slowly she rose half-crouched, her breasts swinging, her face a mask of diabolical hatred. Her fist firmed over the casket. Kandar pushed a little harder.

"Give me the casket, girl, before I disembowel you!"

"You swine's offal! You turd-fed toad! You—" She gasped with the violence of her own hatred. "The casket is mine! I need it! I have planned for this long and long—"

"Give it to me!"

"Listen!" she pleaded desperately. She swallowed. She made some absurdly obscene effort to coquette him, turning her head and smoothing her hair, smiling at him, grimacing. "Listen, stranger. You cannot know what that casket contains—only Tosho and I know the secret. And now Tosho is dead."

Casually, Kandar shattered her hope. "What the casket contains matters nothing to me. I just need it. Hand it over!"

Still she clung to it. She moved her stomach in a writhing gyration away from his sword point. She half fell back, half reclined, grasping the casket to her. "Hear my story, prove you are as great a warrior as you appear! For I have suffered long and long, and this casket will help redress my wrongs."

"Your wrongs mean nothing to me—"

"I was a prisoner of a certain sorcerer whose name I dare not mention for fear of his minion. You know! He wanted me—but I repulsed him and escaped. His black lips! His black gums! His withered hands! Pity me, pity me, for other help now I have none!"

And she looked meaningfully toward the massive silent shape of Krak the Mighty.

"Krak came into my life as a wanderer, a reaver, a wild barbarian from the far western lands. He was strong, strong. He found me, hidden, and treated me well enough, according to his lights. And I induced him, begged him, bribed him with my body, to come here and kill Tosho and take the casket that will bring protection from that certain warlock!"

"I see that," said Kandar, intrigued despite his own imminent affairs. Something was worrying him about this girl, about Krak, and about Tosho.

She caught that indecision with feminine skill. Wriggling a little, she pushed the sword blade to the side. Kandar let it be pushed. She looked up at him, her mouth half-open, the tip of a pink tongue just showing. Lazily, she threw back her head so that her body arched. Her arms lifted behind her head, locked.

"Don't you believe that many men would do—anything—for me?"

Kandar's mouth felt dry and his tongue thick. Abruptly, he saw this girl as a girl, as a desirable girl, whose naked body tempted him like a flame of moonlight in the darkness.

"Krak was a good man, a wild barbarian, but he had no evil in him. And Tosho, poor Tosho of the small talents, trying to make a living caring for the poor people who had not the money to pay for high-powered sorcery, he, too, was a good man."

She licked her lips, her arms buried in the mass of

auburn hair, dark against the ground, the star-glitter through the overarching trees picking out the shine from her eyes, her teeth as she smiled, throwing her white rounded form into a nimbus of sexual allure.

Roughly, Kandar bent, threw down the great sword of Krak, caught at the girl's arm. He pulled.

She came up with his pull, quickly, unexpectedly.

He felt her body against his, soft and firm, her lips on his, wet and caressing, then, with a quick jerk and a mocking laugh, she broke free and ran into the trees. At once he followed. He was after more than the casket now. His character contained a streak of preoccupation with the immediate; he could not forget the plight of his beloved Ferranoz; but there were other pickings in the world, pickings of love and lust he would not miss.

The girl's body flitted between the tree boles.

He caught her with a single bound, leaped on her, knocked her to the ground. Leaves rustled. His arms went about her, and his mouth sought hers. She moved passionately, quickly, to him. "Clumsy, clumsy!" she chided, rolling to the side against his arm, pulling.

He saw the casket gripped in her fist. Through the pounding of lust in his brain and the flushing of heat over his body, he retained sense enough to grab the casket and savagely thrust it down his belt. She laughed shrilly and thrust her body at his face. Warm firm flesh slapped his cheeks. Avidly, he bent forward, and a blinding, sickening pain struck from his groin like lightning splitting an oaktree.

He doubled up, yelling and whooshing.

She flitted away, laughing, her naked white body a flame between the trees.

By the time he had recovered his wind and the pain had subsided to a dull ache, there was nothing to be gained in going after her. He looked back to the clearing and the cave mouth. An hour there to rest and recover would put him in shape for the walk back.

Again that nagging worry about the girl, about Krak and Tosho, gnawed at him. Something he had read in a book, some great idea, would help him now. At least, he had the casket; the girl had saved herself, but she had lost the casket. He touched its bulge under his belt to make sure it was safe.

A strange, wild one, she had been. He had not understood all she had said, for many of her words had been foreign to him. But he had to admire her. He felt sorry for her, too. Had he been a girl, the last person he would want snuffling passionately after him would be Thurdur the Cunning. For that, very obviously, was the certain sorcerer.

He reached the cave mouth and sank down. He felt stiff and sore. Once more that errant memory of something here of importance to him wafted back to his mind. He recalled words written on skins of virgins—words that would *recall*—and then he remembered.

"Of the requisite means of retaining the spirit of a man slain in battle by your own hand—"

The Thaumalogicon had contained that.

That girl, that naked sprite, that witch woman, she had said that both Krak the Mighty and Tosho of the small talents had been good men. He knew with only too close knowledge that Thurdur the Cunning was evil. Yet he had slain both Krak and Tosho in battle at the behest of his own passions and Thurdur's cunning.

As a gentleman, a prince of Akkar, and with the means at hand, he must apologize. He saw nothing strange about his decision. He was light-headed, yes, he knew that. He was near complete exhaustion. He must be seeing things in an askew way. But he had to do what he had to do. He only wished it could be done through the beneficient light of science; as it was, he must once again dabble in the magic arts of thaumaturgy.

He set about gathering the necessary things.

He found fire-lighting implements in Tosho's cave, and soon a small blaze crackled at the cave entrance, a small spit of defiance against the darkness. Over the fire he hung a bronze bowl, scrubbed clean. Then he took up Krak's sword again, hefted it, and walked toward the giant's corpse. For a moment he brooded, looking down, then passed on to where Tosho's head lay among the rocks. He lifted it by the straggling white hair and looked on that wizened face, holding the head up level with eyes.

"Tosho of the small talents," he said.

He put the head in the bronze bowl over the fire.

Then he added to it Krak's head, hewed off with three mighty strokes. He added the hearts of the two men, Krak's mangled, and he added last their genitals, stirring the hideous broth over the hungry fire. When at last all had been consumed and only a thin smoke rose up from the bowl which glowed, he stood up, bracing his legs wide apart, breathing unsteadily.

He leaned over the bowl. The smoke spiraling upwards entered his nostrils and mouth, he smelt and tasted the flat bloody charnel stink of it, and he forced himself to breathe on. Sweat dripped down his face. He had to force himself to stay there, half bent above the bowl, as the last of that fearful brew was consumed.

Slowly, fighting to recall the words with exact accuracy, his brain spinning, his mouth dry and the cesspool stench of the consumed human organs flowing over him like an evil miasma, he repeated the words of power, the words written in *The Thaumalogicon*.

He felt—he knew not what. His limbs were seized with a palsy. He shook. He felt his head seem to expand and shrink. Blinding pains shot through him. He had barely completed the incantation of the spell; he thought he hadn't got it quite right, but he grimly struggled on to grind out the last few words.

The smoke from the bronze bowl ceased.

The fire died down.

He stood there, rigid, unmoving, unable to move, and a strange weird feeling possessed him.

There were many stories of demoniac possession in the rich and varied literature of Akkar, tales of the old gods and the old empires, tales of sorcery that the brain could scarcely comprehend and, if understanding, would shrink from in madness. The sensation of madness came to Kandar of Ferranoz, then, in the nighted woods outside the city of Gilgal where Thurdur the Cunning span his webs of destruction.

"Of the requisite means of *retaining the spirit . . .*"

Kandar had only barely grasped what that meant. He had felt a stupefied almost-drunken sense of sorrow for Krak and Tosho, the aftermath of a struggle to the death

Krak and Tosho, the aftermath of a struggle to the death and of frustrated sexual passion, combining to produce this madness that foamed in his head.

For he heard voices, voices in his head.

Two voices, talking, talking to him, voices querulous and afraid, voices that clamored for understanding.

"If I am dead, then this place is not hell, nor is it sweet Majus' divine abode," said one voice, clear and sharp as a bell in his head. *"What has happened?"*

And the other voice, the other voice boomed; "By the diseased left testicle of Kragunoth! I know not where we are, little man, but I would like the feel of my true blade, Koztivkure in my hand, for I think I have never been afraid before in all my life."

"Krak the Mighty!" exclaimed Kandar, screaming with the impossibility of what was happening to him. "Tosho of the small talents! Alive! In my head!"

"Who calls us?" Both voices blended, the great boom and the querulous squeak.

"I am Kandar of Ferranoz," thought Kandar. "I am the man who slew you both."

"Aye!" rumbled the bass boom. "A good fight, and a clever one. But I am dead! You skewered me like a piglet—how, then, can I hear you and talk to you, and how can this squeaking midget Tosho also hear and talk to us? us?"

Tosho's voice said quickly; "I have heard—even I, with my small talents, have heard—what the higher necromancy can accomplish. I have heard of *The Ochre Scroll*—"

"This spell," interrupted Kandar gently, "came from *The Thaumalogicon.*"

"Powerful! Powerful!" came Tosho's whisper.

"This squeaking star-begotten wizard may understand!" boomed Krak's mighty voice. "But I do not! We fought, you and I, Kandar of Ferranoz! We fought and I am dead and all the spells in Golden Rathvane would not bring me back to life!"

"Only your spirit, which the enchantment allows me to retain, that is all, Krak. I do not pretend to understand all myself. But I can talk to you, you can talk to me—"

Tosho's voice broke in, suddenly, shrill. "I see! I see my own cave mouth, a fire, my bronze bowl—I see it through another's eyes—through the eyes of Kandar of Ferranoz!"

"Aye, aye," grumbled Krak. "I see, too. So the cocksparrow killed you, too, did he?"

"I did not—that is, I—" Kandar stumbled. How could he explain? He felt the nearness of these two men, the solidity of their presence within him, their spirit with his. He felt them as friendly, warm men he would have been proud to own as friends. But he had killed them both. He began a stumbling reply when he felt a strange hollowness within him, a sudden sensation like a lamp blowing out in a cavern of bats.

"Krak! Tosho!" he called.

Their voices swirled back, conjoined, counterpointed, diminishing.

"We cannot see! We are being drawn back—away—Kandar of Ferranoz, hold us, for through you we yet live—"

"Come back!" Kandar screamed into the vault of his own skull. "Krak the Mighty! Tosho of the small talents! Return! By the powers of the enchantment, I command you! Return to me!"

But only emptiness and silence lay on the other side of his mind.

Chapter Six

Of The Ochre Scroll *and the strange fight on the stairs*

The sky displayed a pre-dawn flush and the treetops barely moved against the rising glow when Kandar of Ferranoz, Lion of Akkar, stepped out into the clearing. He felt rested. After that inexplicable departure of the two slain men from his mind he had fallen into a sleep more unconsciousness than true sleep, to drift gently into a slumber that left him, now he had awakened, ready to meet what must come at Thurdur the Cunning's tower.

He called out, hard and strong: "Thurdur the Cunning!"

He waited for Myder's arrival with the flying bench. He wished he'd had presence of mind enough to have asked Tosho what was the significance of the casket. The strange foreign girl had known. She claimed it gave her immunity from Thurdur. He waited. Myder and the flying bench did not come.

Purposefully, thinking, Kandar set off for Gilgal.

As he walked with his springy stride through the forest and out along the open countryside, he wondered whether he dared use the casket's power against Thurdur. But his own sense of cunning led him to the true answer.

Protection against Thurdur the jade casket might give; but it would not induce him to part with the secrets of *The Ochre Scroll*. And those secrets Kandar meant to have.

He walked still untired in through the gate and directly to the Tower of Taractacus. Here guards let him in with an immediate obsequious air he found amusing—and memory-stirring.

The air struck chill at him as he tramped surrounded by guards up marble staircases and along draughty tapestried corridors. The air struck damp; the air struck with a horror he had to brace himself to face.

The city of Gilgal that ruled the lands from the Langaan Hills to the sea was ruled in turn by an evil spirit pent in the debased guise of Thurdur the Cunning. Kandar of Ferranoz held his back lance-straight as he stalked into that ebon chamber of wizardry.

Myder's light, as before, shone eerily on the ranked artifacts of sorcery. Every window was close-shuttered. The air smelled dank and unwholesome. Thurdur the Cunning started up from a fusty daybed dragged to the center of the chamber. He looked excited, bent over, rubbing his gnarled hands together.

"Well! Well!" he snuffled eagerly. "Give it to me!"

Kandar closed his hand over the casket. "First you

must let me see *The Ochre Scroll!*"

Angrily, his blackened gums and yellowed teeth gnashing, Thurdur lifted a hand, pointed a finger, began to intone a spell. Then he stopped, shaking and trembling so that his robes shook wildly, as Myder lunged forward between Thurdur and his victim.

"Master!" screeched that honed voice. "Remember, he has the casket!"

"Yes, yes, Myder! Of course!"

Clearly, Kandar saw, in his anger Thurdur had forgotten the casket and would have hurled a spell at Kandar. Then, the protection the foreign girl had spoken of would have acted. A stronger emotion took hold of Kandar.

"While I hold the casket you cannot harm me! Very well, then. Show me the book!"

Fiercely and venomously, with many a fiendish glare, Thurdur the Cunning opened the great dragonskin-bound tome and placed it on a table so that Kandar, by leaning over the wizard, could read the ancient writing.

Myder's light made the writing jump and leap, and Kandar was grimly reminded of the static light of burning Ferranoz by which he had read the companion book to this. Feverishly, he turned to the pages at the end, the pages separately locked and bound The lock did not open.

He pointed.

"Open me this section, Thurdur, for here I know is the information about the greater intelligences I must have!"

Thurdur spat dryly. His clawed fingers fumbled like a spider over its prey, holding the ebon key, thrusting it into the lock, turning with a sharp squeal like that of a rat whose back is broken in a trap.

"Read, boy! And much good may it do you! For the greater intelligences are mighty beyond your comprehension. They will chew up your land of Akkar and spit it out like a pumpkin seed!"

Grimly, determined, Kandar read on. He found a number of spells with which, partially, he was familiar. A terrible suspicion began to burn in his brain.

Desperately he read on. He saw once again the spell to retain a man's spirit slain in battle—and he saw at once the items he had omitted when he had intoned the spell by the flickering firelight at the cave's mouth. Other spells he but flicked over, reading their names and passing on, not committing all their details to memory, racing on like a demented maniac toward the end, seeking faster and ever more frenziedly for the spells that would summon the greater intelligences.

He reached the endpaper and stared sickly at the imprimatur of a bloody skull with the lily clenched in its gappy teeth. That symbol ended the book. There was no more. And now Thurdur the Cunning was reaching with eager trembling fingers for the jade casket, was fumbling in a ghoulish clawing at his belt.

Once Kandar passed over that casket, all defense against the sorceries of Thurdur would be lost.

Myder's light flared up brightly, showing the gleaming light of madness reflected in Thurdur's faded eyes. His narrow face looked skull-like, his groping hands skeletal.

"Give me the casket, boy!"

Instinctively Kandar flinched back.

He remembered he was a gentleman, a Prince of Akkar, and yet—and yet—he had given his word and must honor that promise—and yet—and yet—

"There is nothing in this tawdry *Ochre Scroll* that will help my beloved city of Ferranoz! It's all the same, all the same as before."

Shaking with eagerness, Thurdur advanced like a toad as Kandar retreated. "Not the same, boy. I have seen a copy of *The Thaumalogicon*. The spell's similar in each; but the order is different. *Give me the casket!*"

"You gave your word!" shrieked the knife-voice of Myder.

"I did give my word . . ." faltered Kandar. He grasped the casket as a man sucked into a bog grasps a blade of grass.

"Give me the casket!"

Shrinking from that baleful glare, those black gums and yellow teeth, those writhing black lips, that outstretched claw hand, Kandar stumbled back to the table, put out a hand to steady himself. The other hand, holding the casket, he reached out to Thurdur.

"Here—" he began.

"No!" shrieked a voice in his brain. *"Don't give him the casket!"*

In that frightful moment Kandar surely thought he had gone mad.

A voice, in his head, screaming at him!

Then another voice, a deep booming bass, roared; "By the pink left nipple of sweet Vashtilulu the Buxom! I feel you have Koztivkure slung on your back! Strike down the foul wizard, and have done!"

"Aye," squeaked Tosho, "for what he had you do to me, do as Krak says, and strike his blasphemous head from his loathsome shoulders!"

Krak and Tosho! There, in his head, their spirits speaking to him as friends!

He drew back his hand.

At once Thurdur started back, his hand flung up, his face a writhing pit of hell-displayed.

"Give me the casket, you petty poxed princeling, or I'll blast you to a crawling worm where you stand!"

Kandar hefted the casket. "Not while I hold this! I'll honor my bargain with you—but I'll also take leave to protect my life. Only when I am safely away from this awful place shall you take the casket!"

"Strike him down!" boomed Krak's mental voice.

"No, no," counseled Tosho, suddenly cautious. "For the casket confers only protection against Thurdur's wizardry. He can protect himself against a clumsy sword with the greatest ease—"

"Clumsy sword, did you say?" rumbled Krak. "I'll have you know Koztivkure is as sweetly balanced as any blade in the Eleven Kingdoms! By the cavernous navel of sweet Vashtilulu the Buxom! There never was a sword as deft as Koztivkure!"

"Our Kandar finds it difficult to swing, barbarian!" snapped back Tosho.

"He's a stripling! A milk-pudding mother's boy! When he's fleshed out a bit, I'll show him the tricks of the trade."

Kandar, gripping the casket, glared at with concentrated hatred by the faded demoniac eyes of Thurdur and the brilliant orbs of Myder, backed slowly toward the door.

"I think," friend Krak," he said mentally, "that at this rather interesting juncture—" His hand fell to the hilt of the bandit sword—"I'll stick to the blade I can wield." He could not refrain from adding, "You, of all men, know that I can wield it with some skill."

Krak's mental belch sounded like a hippo kicked between wind and water. "I'll grant you that, Our Kandar. I'll give you the credit for being a master swordsman." Kandar backed from the door, the blade now naked in his hand, the casket tucked back into his belt. "But," went on Krak with a fine free indignation; "If my foot hadn't turned on that stone, you'd never have pinked me."

Guardsmen raced up the long curved flight of stairs outside Thurdur's door. They wore white tunics and white trousers gathered at the ankles. Their steel caps were heavily chased and engraved, with nasals and tall spiked plumes of scarlet and green. Each man brandished a curved scimitar in his right hand, his left holding a small round bronze targe.

"Sword fodder!" roared Krak's huge voice in Kandar's mind. "Charge them! Sweep them away like puffballs!"

"I am not built as you, Krak. I have not your weight—"

There was no time, now, for the irony of that remark to sink in. In a flash of bright reflected light and a clang of steel, the blades engaged. Two guards attacked Kandar simultaneously. He had no trouble with the right-hand one; a low semi-stopped thrust through the belly where there were no bones to impede immediate withdrawal disposed of him. But left-hand Charlie swung his shield first and slashed diagonally with his curved blade.

"*Duck!*" came the stentorian bellow in Kandar's mind.

Obediently, Kandar ducked.

The scimitar chewed away a handful of his hair and left a long shallow gouge across his scalp.

"There! You see!" yelled Kandar in a rage. "That was no place to duck! What I ought to have done was— this——and this—and that—"

Three lightning thrusts sent the guards toppling, left-hand Charlie staring stupidly at his life-blood oozing out onto his white clothes.

"Well," boomed Krak. "That'll do—"

"Here come more guards!" chittered Tosho. "Why don't you leave Our Kandar to get on with the fight? He knows what he's doing."

"By the black polluted heart of Kragunoth! Can't I offer professional advice?" He sounded mightily indignant and chafing to be active during a fight.

"If only you could throw a spell at them!" Tosho, too, sounded pent-up and frustrated.

Kandar could not hold an enchantment in his mind at this split-up time of violent action, when his sword rang and clanged and slithered against the scimitars of the guards, when bright blood spurted, when men screamed their death agonies. A spell? He couldn't think of one right now . . .

In his mind Tosho's squeaky voice screamed; "Say after me, Kandar, repeat my words exactly, you need not think what they mean."

"All right," grunted Kandar, clattering down the first flight of stairs. If he was to fight his way out of this ebony tower then he'd best get started. "Say on."

Krak's bull bellow smashed over Tosho's beginning squeak.

"This is no time for sorcery! Don't spell, *sword!*"

If only, Kandar thought with unhappy fury, *if only instead of swords or sorcery I could employ the bright light of science now!*

His blade, shining silver no longer but shining crimson, slid in and out, turned, struck, cut and slashed. Blood stained his own blue tunic and trousers. His snake-booted feet felt carefully for every purchase on the blood-stained marble. As he descended that wide marble stairway he left a grisly trail of huddled white-clad bodies, gorily stained, abandoned in the lax postures of death.

Tosho spoke the words in his mind that he must repeat.

He could not understand them. They seemed mere arbitrary words in nonsensical order. ". . . stomach of pain the dispel . . ."

He shouted them aloud, in time to his rhythmical weavings and turnings, his sword blurring to slip past bronze shield and brandished scimitar.

He heard Krak's gasp in his mind.

The giant's voice rumbled angrily, "By Crox! *Archers!*"

Where the staircase swept down below the upper floor a balcony jutted. Poised on the sweep of railed flooring, a half-score of archers aimed the arrows from their deeply curved reflex bows toward the leaping Kandar.

He carried on that leap; like a feral half-tamed beast of the jungle he crashed soldiers to the marble, using their prostrate bodies as stepping stones down the stairs. He swung the sword in a crimson-flying circle about him. Arrows skittered past his shoulder to plink onto the marble or to thud fleshily into prostrate guards.

He rounded the curve of staircase, with Krak's great voice mentally urging him on, still himself yelling those nonsensical words of Tosho's aloud.

A fresh group of archers ran into view on the court below, where the stairs debouched. A full score this time, the first half-score knelt to aim their shafts up as their comrades of the second half-score released their arrows from a standing position toward the leaping Kandar, shouting and brandishing his sword.

He ducked. Reflexes took over. Bent over, he snatched up a fallen round bronze targe, snapped it up into position. Only a single arrow struck it, to glance off with a savage whine. The other arrows smacked into the pursuing white-clad guards. He heard screams and obscene gurglings from up the stairs, but he did not look around.

For he had finished the chant dictated to him by Tosho, and now he looked keenly for the next arrow flight from that second half-score of bowmen.

But the bowmen did not shoot. They doubled up in agony. They cast away their bows. Screams and howls dinned out over the courtyard to mingle with the shrieks from the dying above.

"What's happening, by Helios, what's going on?"

Other guards, over by the main gates, were crumpling to the ground. Their faces turned green; they vomited, they lay on their sides, legs drawn up, and howled in anguish.

Tosho laughed with elfin spiteful glee, there in Kandar's mind.

"I have small talents; I cure the country people, who come to me because they dislike the high sorcery. By the shed blood of sweet Majus, our day will come again!"

"By the supple hips of sweet Vashtilulu the Buxom!" roared Krak. "Get us out of here, Kandar, before they recover from Tosho's tricks and rip us up from navel to breakfast-time! Stir yourself, boy!"

Not needing the bidding, Kandar ran for the gate. It stood with the wicket open and a dozen clumped guards about it, rolling and writhing as they grasped their stomachs and howled As he raced through, Kandar heard in his mind the ghostly tinkle of Tosho's wicked laughter.

"A simple spell, Our Kandar, a country magic to cure a yokel's stomach-ache—but intoned backwards, it brings on the aches! You saw! A small magic—"

"By Dangorn! A small talent but a potent one, Tosho! You saved our bacon then!"

"And stir your stumps, Our Kandar," interrupted Krak, "or you'll get us all killed yet. Those women-clad soldier-lads will be after us without delay."

Fleetly, Kandar ran from that shadow-haunted tower of horror.

No incongruity affected him, or Krak or Tosho, over their desire not to be killed—men already dead and now sharing an eerie half-life by courtesy of their slayer—for they *did* now live, and if Kandar died they would be truly dead.

The narrow streets of Gilgal swallowed him like a dung beetle in a stable.

He slowed to a quick walk, turned in to a narrow bazaar and, brushing past garishly decorated stalls, their lamps alight and flaring in the morning dimness off the crowded streets beneath the overhanging balconies, he pushed through to the inn where he had left the horses. They were still there, and the stableman for a few copper coins brought them out, rubbed down and fed and watered, ready to be off.

Kandar had no fear of what the landlord of his customers might say, should he decide to stroll into the inn, about the man who had been summoned by Thurdur the Cunning in so ghastly a way, astride a Myder-directed bench; but there was no time now for pleasantries.

About to mount he paused with his hand on the saddle pommel. A second stableman was bringing out animals from other stalls. Kandar stared. He had never seen animals like this before. He thought he might have heard of them in traveler's tales, so he stared with the country-bumpkin curiosity of a boy who, although a prince, was still finding his way in the wide world beyond Akkar.

70

"By Ganchi! What manner of beast are they?"

Tosho answered, impatiently, irritably. "Haven't you ever seen a Dumarest before? Though they don't often come down this far south at this time of the year. They like hot weather."

The reason for that was easily seen. Each Dumarest had a skin without hairs on the body. The size of a powerful horse, with four legs shod with bright metal, the animal's body curved up for another two feet or so from the front legs. The head was poised intelligently on the neck and, immediately below this, the shoulders supported a pair of small arms. The Dumarest was not, Kandar realized, comparable with that fabled beast of antiquity that combined horse's and a man's body; but it did create a bizarre impression.

"Never seen a Dumarest before, hey, lad!" boomed a cheerful voice in his ear. For a moment Kandar thought it was Krak; then he turned to see one of the hunters he had last seen drinking and dicing in the tavern. His three companions were with him. Their broad-brimmed hats with the brightly colored bird plumage drooping from them splashed brilliance into the stable yard.

"Interesting animals," observed Kandar.

The hunter's eyes narrowed to mere blue slits. He glared at Kandar, and his right hand whipped up to the hilt of the rapier carried high on his back.

"I recognize you! You were carried from hence—on a bench!"

"May Bright Gyrane strike him down!" called a hunter.

These men could not mention the name ringing in all their ears; but they didn't like sorcery—that was clearly evident as four long blades whickered out and Kandar faced four points held unerringly on his heart.

"Now wait a minute—" he began.

"Don't argue, ninny!" Krak's massive voice bellowed in Kandar's brain. "Clear your steel—or you'll be dead, and us with you!"

Tearing out the bandit sword, Kandar shouted, "I have no quarrel with you. Let me go peacefully about my business! I am no sorcerer!"

Tosho's alarmed squeak sobered him. "More's the pity, Our Kandar! Use a spell on 'em, lad!"

The blades met in a ringing clangor.

"I can't remember a spell now!" shouted Kandar, exasperated. "Isn't that obvious? You tell me what to say to make 'em sick again, Tosho!"

He backed up, swinging the bandit sword with its slight curvature in what he at once recognized was a clumsy defense against the snake-licking thrusts of the rapiers. These hunters fought well, professionally, with no time out for false heroics He was pressed hard. He gave more ground. His foot struck a wooden bucket of water, and he stumbled back.

Four rapier points thrust for his heart.

Those four needle-sharp points halted a bare thumb's breadth above his panting chest. The leader of the four, a man of bronzed face and long blond mustaches, with the wrinkles of laughter and good living lending his face a jovial openness, considered.

"He's no sorcerer, comrades. If he was, he'd have spelled us sooner than being spitted like a porker for the roast." He bent down and took Kandar's left hand. "Up with you, my lad."

A little shamefacedly, Kandar scrambled up. He, the best swordsman in all Akkar, bested by four rapier-armed hunters from some barbarian northern land! Really, he didn't know what had come over him.

A light step in the stable yard took their attention.

Here came the fifth member, the one they had been waiting for last night.

Kandar just gaped.

She was slender and firm, dressed as were the hunters in brown leather; but hers had been cut and drawn fine to her figure, so that Kandar could admire trim legs and a waist sculpted for arm-crooking. Her brown hair fell in luxurious waves to her shoulders. Her face, coppery with health, straight-nosed, firm-chinned, lifted like a glowing flower of the fields to Kandar. Hazel eyes regarded him coolly.

"A brawl, Alleyn?" she said sideways. You know how that sort of oafish behavior disgusts me." She kept looking at Kandar.

Alleyn, the leader, began a low chuckle, instantly stilled as the girl turned her small head to look at him.

"Nothing serious, my lady," he said evenly.

She turned back to Kandar. He felt the regard of those hazel eyes on him, the force of her personality flowing over as a flooded stream flows over and engulfs a weaker creek.

"I am the Lady Angelena of Ascapard."

Kandar opened his mouth and then, cautious, shut it again. He had shouted his reckless challenge at Myder in the tavern last night; but from the rough behavior of the huntsmen he reasoned either they had not heard or understood his titles, or they had not believed. Either way, no need to betray himself to a possible kidnapping.

"I am Kandar," he said.

She lifted one thinly penciled eyebrow.

"We ride to Grimwald and thence northwards. What is your road, Kandar?"

He hesitated.

Krak's coarse chuckle in his head and Tosho's thin giggle infuriated him. Even his sex life was no longer his own!

"I also ride north," he said gruffly.

Alleyn's heavy voice boomed. "Address my lady with due civility, my lad, or you'll feel my rapier point tickle you where you jump!"

She inclined her head, her hazel eyes liquidly drawing him on, her mouth curved in a closed half-smile very annoying to a young man anxious to show his prowess.

"Thank you, good Alleyn. Now, let us mount, all!"

Kandar swung a long leg over his horse's saddle. The hunters and their lady mounted their Dumarests with supple ease, the mounts turning their heads and with their small upper arms assisting their riders to their seats. The men made small whistling noises to the Dumarests, who responded in a similar way. Kandar's flesh crawled. The humans were conversing with their animals!

In a click-clopping-click procession, they trotted out of the inn yard.

"Well, now what you have landed yourself in?" demanded Tosho querulously. "What's wrong with you, Our Kandar?"

As the afternoon lazed along, Kandar told Krak and Tosho what had happened to him since the gray wolfling horde had descended on Dreaming Ferranoz at the behest of some inimical intelligences. "And now I must seek the means to summon to my aid those benign intelligences who will help us!"

"I have seen Thurdur's *Ochre Scroll,* for at one time I assisted him," mused Tosho. "The thaumaturgy there is too powerful for one of my small talents. But I do know of the benign intelligences you seek; beings less, it is true, than the Beneficient Lord Majus, but beings able to achieve that which you require."

"You know?" rumbled Krak.

"A dying man babbled out the secret of his life, one day long ago, told me of the lost and secret tomb of the famous wizard Nga-ereshvigal, servant of the Lord of Shadows, warlock, necromancer—and possessor of *The Umbre Testament!*"

A flare of excitement died in Kandar.

"It'll be the same as the others, the same old spells but in a different order. What has—?"

"The same, yes, but!" shrilled Tosho, impassioned at his host's obtuseness. "But there must be a reason for the three books to be called *The Trilogos Damnae!* And we must press on, for Thurdur will be lusting to take possession of his jade casket. Press on north, Our Kandar!"

Chapter Seven

In which despite Monkey-Ghouls and the misuse of an Enchantment my Lady Angelena of Ascapard was kind to Kandar of Ferranoz.

The Kingdom of Taractea extended from the huge jumbled expanse of broken rocks, upland plateaus and jutting peaks collectively called the Langaan Hills right away to the sea, here called not the Sea of Dreams but the Western Ocean. Many leagues northwards lay the border of Taractea. Kandar felt uneasily sure that Thurdur the Cunning would strike there.

Tosho kept urging all haste. Krak grumbled about being in sore need of a fight. Kandar, obstinately, during the succeeding days, kept pace with the Lady Angelena and her four hunters. They kept themselves very much to themselves at night-time halts at lonely inns, but Kandar felt that strong sexual allure streaming from the copper-flowing girl. One day they were riding late, aiming for Grimwald at nightfall.

The hunters, following their leader Alleyn's guidance, seemed to have accepted him now, although they still gave him puzzled looks from time to time. Kandar felt ravenous. His tiredness he could keep at bay, but he felt as though his stomach was cuddling up to his backbone.

When, during the afternoon, they halted at a wayside inn on the road and the hunters and Angelena took merely a light repast, Kandar ordered up and devoured a feast of a meal. He paid with good grace, hardly caring that his purse contained a few silver coins, a handful of coppers and a single golden Dotus. On that golden coin was beautifully engraved the head of his father. There were few men in the world who could say that about a coin.

It made him think, made him tuck into his meal, made him determined to find *The Umbre Testament* and so unlock the mystery of *The Trilogy of the Damned*.

Toward evening, when the long blue afternoon turned gradually into a rose and pinkish-green evening afterglow, they saw before them a dark forest athwart the road.

"The forest of Semele," called the lady Angelena to Kandar. "Grimwald lies directly beyond it, a mere three leagues." She moved gracefully in her seat, her face sharp against the horizon glow, her luxurious hair shadowed. "Some say it is enchanted," she finished casually.

Alleyn chuckled harshly.

Tosho squeaked, "Grimwald lies at the border."

Kandar replied, "I have given my word."

Krak rumbled, "By the diseased left testicle of Kragunoth! I suppose you have, boy!"

"I'm not very happy about it," snapped back Kandar.

75

"What about this lady Angelena and her men?" asked Tosho.

"If he doesn't know what to do about her—" roared Krak joyfully in Kandar's skull. "By the lecherous eyes of sweet Vashtilulu the Buxom I'll soon show him!"

"Like you treated—" began Tosho. But the wizard of the small talent's voice thinned and dwindled. Krak's mighty bellow in answering rage at the accusation faded and dimmed. A black void clapped like a hollow bell in Kandar's mind. He felt panic. His friends had gone! Once more, inexplicably, Krak and Tosho had gone.

"Do you feel all right, Kandar?"

The lady Angelena's anxious voice roused him. He sat up in the saddle. He smiled.

"Perfectly, your lady. I merely dozed."

"Not the best of times to doze," she rallied him acidly. "Riding through the forest of Semele. Keep your eyes open."

"For what?"

Alleyn bent to the linen-wrapped bundle suspended from his saddle. "Everything," he said, harshly. He took out a crossbow, ready strung, and began to wind it up with the cranequin, with casual expertise bracing the bow against his Dumarest and saddle, turning as though he was grinding corn.

The other hunters did the same.

All Kandar could do was loosen his sword in its scabbard.

The lady Angelena turned a half-smiling face to him.

"You carry a large weapon, Kandar."

He refused to be drawn. Right now he was too concerned about Tosho and Krak.

"It is a memento," he said curtly.

Her eyes measured him. He knew what she meant. He hefted Koztivkure into a more comfortable position on his back. Come to think of it, it might be easier to wield from a horse's back. He'd have to try it if he got the opportunity, and riding through this dark and gloomy forest looked to be a fine time to start.

A Dumarest whistled with nerve-tingling alarm.

From the trees leggy banded shapes dropped like a swarming host of demon monkeys from the vaults of hell.

Banded in black and brown and orange fur, they poured in a surging tide from the trees. Their sharp teeth glittered in the last roseate drops of sunshine, flung and scattered through the trees like blood, and their eyes reflected that sanguinary glow. They carried sharp notched spears, and cunning little knives that curved in a double loop. They screeched and chittered and flung themselves on the benighted travelers.

Crossbow strings thunked. Four quarrels found targets. But the little monsters rolled on over their dead fellows. Four rapiers scraped scabbards. Kandar drew his bandit sword; Krak's mighty Koztivkure would not, in Kandar's hands, be fast or nimble enough for this work.

His mouth felt dry. He recognized the odds. Then he saw the lady Angelena, looking as cool as lettuced butter, wielding her own long rapier with masterly swordswomanship.

One of the hunters was down, tiny teeth fastened in his jugular. He died swiftly, on a gurgle. The Dumarests were fighting, too, their small forelimbs slashing short swords about and slicing up flying furry bodies.

A second hunter went down. For a horrific instant Kandar caught a glimpse of his rapier with four furry bodies impaled on it like kebabs, but all wriggling and chittering, before he vanished behind them. For now the Dumarests were galloping hard along the forest trail, with Kandar's four horses in fierce pursuit. He flailed away with his sword, more knocking away the furry horrors than swording them off. Alleyn's Dumarest screamed shrilly as a spear tore into its upper body. Alleyn catapulted out of the saddle and his flying body struck a tree branch hanging above the trail. Kandar was fiercely engaged, and the next time he looked he thought he saw Alleyn feebly moving in the crotch of the trunk and branch, but fresh spears flashed toward him and he could not be sure.

Then the lady Angelena of Ascapard went down.

Immediately, without thought, her last remaining huntsman dived after her. Spears ribboned him as he sprawled over his mistress. The Dumarests, whistling shrilly, milled and then, a second one brought cruelly down, the remaining two galloped away.

The four horses reached where a dead man lay half

across a girl. The trail was now very dark. Twice, now, Kandar had struck at a small agile body and caught it squarely; twice the animals had failed to avoid his blow. So they didn't see so well in the night, huh? Kandar slid off the horses's back, still holding to the pommel and with his foot in the stirrup. He bent down with his free arm, riding the horse from the side. He had not gone down after the girl unthinkingly, as had her huntsman.

He scooped her up, giving the dead man a tumbling nose dive into the trees.

The horse, responding, galloped heavily down the trail. The other three followed, snorting. With the lady Angelena cradled clumsily in his left arm, he smashed two, three, four quick sword-blows away at the few viciously struggling monkey-ghouls who clung on. He felt teeth razor across his shoulder, near Angelena's head and his right arm and hand brought the bandit sword so rapidly across that the point gouted out from the wriggling banded body. It almost—almost but not quite—burrowed on into Angelena's flesh.

Kandar drew a deep shuddering breath. He had not forgotten Elthalee. He had never forgotten that fatal javelin-cast. He would never forget. But almost—almost he had wounded a girl in his care again.

He looked down on Angelena. Her head twisted sideways and she looked up at him. In her coppery face was a look of sensuous enjoyment. Her hazel eyes stared up at him. She was reveling with a voluptuous passion in the danger. She smiled at him; not an enigmatic half-smile, but a full, wide, seductive, all-consuming smile of shared understanding.

Then the horse crashed over a projecting tree root and somersaulted all asprawl into the tree.

There was no time for dizziness. Scurrying feet pattered after them. Frenziedly, Kandar scooped up Angelena and plunged with her in his arms into the forest. He ran crookedly, all his enormous strength exerted in just staying up and running.

Two of the black and brown and orange-banded horrors had spotted his flight. They ran fleetly after him, chittering. He roughly slung Angelena over his left shoulder. Her face blazed with reckless excitement. The bandit sword flicked in! out! with superb poise. The first monkey-ghoul went down, blood as black as ink spouting in the gloom. The second little horror jabbed his spear at Kandar's genitals. He blocked the blow, then struck down.

The blade hit the ghoul-monkey's head and jerked. The beast went down; but the bandit sword was firmly lodged in the remains of a bronze cap and the beast's shattered skull. Kandar put a foot on the thing's body and pulled. Footsteps and chittering rose about him.

"Go on!" whispered Angelena. "Leave that sword. If they come again, you'll have to use your bigger weapon!" Her eyes showed feverish lust.

Relinquishing the weapon with a pang, for the bandit sword had been a good friend to him, Kandar ran on into the concealing gloom of the trees.

Fragments of spells danced and jumbled in his brain.

He tried with despairing effort to hold just one, to concentrate the words, to capture the concept entire.

"By Thothak and by Mumulak, let the bones of their sinews—no! No! That's not it!"

Gasping with mental as much as physical torture he rushed on, brushing through underbrush and prickly thorn bushes tearing his clothes, feeling cloth rip and part. Angelena cried out, a short, sharp cry of pain.

He halted at once. All about him he could hear the night murmurs of the forest. He strained his ears. Nothing. He could hear no sounds of pursuit. Angelena wriggled, and he set her down clumsily. Her brown leathers were torn. Then, harsh, harrowingly, a chittering cry wailed up.

"The monkey-ghouls!" whispered Angelena. Her breasts heaved. Her face glowed, there in the dimness, her hazel eyes large and excited.

Kandar scooped her up again and crashed on. Thickets reached thorny arms for him. He ran until the sweat glistened down his bared chest, cutting swathes through the blood spouted there from dying little horrors.

His foot caught under a tree root. Headlong, the girl in his arms, he pitched down. Branches clashed about him. They lay in a leaf-filled hollow beneath the spread roots of a great tree, with thorny underbrush clicking back over them. Rips showed on Kandar's flesh. A single star pierced a narrow beam of light down. In that dim almost nonexistent light he saw her face, laughing, aglow, fiercely exalted.

He started to rise and she gripped him, dragged him down.

"Stay, Kandar! Keep silent! Here —we are safe."

She bent her head so that her hair fell about him and fastened her hot lips to his. Surprised, dizzied, filled with passionate energy, he responded. The kiss brought a tingling flame burning in his loins.

She drew back. She quickly unlaced her leather tunic, drew it down and off. Beneath, she was naked. Her body, shadowed, dim, vague, smelled warm and healthy and heavy with promise. Without thinking, Kandar pulled her closer to him, buried his head in her bosom, kissed her breasts with an abandon she shared and enhanced. Her head thrown back now, her eyes wide and staring, her hands clawing at his back, she responded like a magnificent pagan animal.

Silently, they made love, there beneath the thorn bushes and the roots of the great tree, while all about them crept the stealthy chittering forms of the monkey-ghouls.

The dead leaves had formed a soft, warm mold. Kandar experienced no discomfort. When it was over, he sat up breathing deeply and feeling wonderful. The great sword Koztivkure lay at his side. Smiling secretly, one hand pushing her hair back from her flushed face, the lady Angelena touched the sword with her other hand.

"I knew it," she said languorously. Her passion might have frightened Kandar in other circumstances.

"I—" he said, stumblingly.

She drew the remnants of her tunic about her shoulders.

"No, dear Kandar. Nothing more need lie between us. While you have this great sword, you and I shall be friends."

He nodded dumb.

Furtive sounds filtered down to them. The tops of the trees moved now, soughing, making it difficult to pick out and identify the smaller hostile sounds of the monkey-ghouls.

"Apsalothoc stalks the forests," she said, with a little shiver. "It must be midnight."

"Alleyn said . . ." he began. "You do not believe in sorcery in your land?"

She smiled. "Believe? Who can not believe when you see thaumaturgy employed so freely? But we do not employ the Black Arts."

"The Black Arts?" interrupted Kandar, amazed and annoyed. "I'm not talking about those silly, spooky devil-callings. They are fit for diseased minds. I am speaking of the conscious use of enchantment."

"So your sort claim—"

"My sort?" It was his turn to smile, bitterly. "I would far rather employ the blessed light of science. But circumstances force me to use sorcery to find the answer to the riddle that will unlock the ensorcelled city of Dreaming Ferranoz!"

He explained.

"And now I must seek the lost tomb of Nga-ereshvigal, servant of the Lord of Shadows. There I hope to find a copy of *The Umbre Testament.*"

She shivered suddenly at his last words and drew closer to him. From the forest the sound of Apsalothoc soughed from the tree tops.

"I can help you, Kandar—Prince Kandar Heliodotus—"

"Kandar."

"Away to the west, across the Western Ocean, lies the island of Histiaea. As a child, I listened to stories from my guardians of the pursuit and slaying of Nga-ereshvigal. There, on the enchanted Isle of Histiaea, lies his tomb, lost and secret and forgotten."

Hope flared in Kandar.

"But," went on Angelena, "I do not know if this is true, or merely a fable spun from moonbeams to entrance a fretful child."

"It's got to be true!" snarled Kandar.

He recalled how reluctant Krak had been to tell him of the mighty barbarian's origins. From the far west, was all Krak would say. Far out, across the shining ocean, other lands lay, so everyone believed. The Isle of Histiaea. Well. If the tomb of Nga-ereshvigal existed, Kandar would find it. He promised that to Helios, with a temple down by the riverbank, a temple of twenty slender white columns and roof of plated gold over bronze. By Helios, yes!

"But you," Angelena whispered. "You can conjure sorceries?"

"I try." Abruptly, Kandar felt abashed. "I try."

Could he try to call Kholokova or Sassilinja to aid him now? The spells were long and involved, and he had thought them branded on his brain; but the trick was to hold the spell entire. He glanced at the warm coppery aliveness of Angelena. No. He must attempt a smaller magic now.

He remembered a page of archaic writing, written on the skin of a virgin. Memory of Angelena's warm skin against his flesh, of the scent of her hair, the feel of her firmly soft body in his arms, spurred him on, made him strong with his own strength. He began to intone the words that would conjure fire and smoke and blow them down the wind.

". . . roiling on the flame winds of puissant Dangorn and burning with an unconsuming fire . . ."

He was a man of a few tattered spells, remnants and scraps of arcane knowledge, trying to use his thaumaturgical powers in face of the great unknown.

A wind grew, a wind that rivaled Apsalothoc. A spark flashed into being. Another. And another. Flames enwrapped a tree beyond the thorn bushes. Fire burst out with a crackling roar. Like savage beasts howling as the cage doors fly up, the flames leaped out. Vivid tongues and gouts of flame lambently blazed up. The forest burned.

"What have you done?" screamed Angelena.

"Up!" shouted Kandar, roughly. He had not expected this. Once more a spell had played him false.

They began to run through the forest, northwards, away from the flames, flitting through the aisles of the forest. Wildly they leaped fallen tree trunks, scrambled through thorn brakes, splashed through secret winding streams. Through the crackle of flames and the enchanted flame winds breathed by puissant Dangorn they heard the insane chittering.

"The monkey-ghouls are running!" gasped Angelena.

"You run, save your breath!" answered Kandar, dragging her on.

82

Panting for breath, they slowed to a fast walk and pressed on, feeling their way through the trees, with all the sky alight where they had been. They kept on going, heading north, heading for Grimwald, and heading, as Kandar had somberly determined, for the lost tomb of Ngaereshvigal, servant of the Lord of Shadows, one-time owner of the accursed tome, *The Umbre Testament.*

A poor fool among sorcerers he might be, but he held the true blade Koztivkure, a lissom girl wanted his love, he rejoiced in the friendship of two ghostly spirits, and he would sell his soul to make amends for his failure when Dreaming Ferranoz fell into that enchanted sleep.

Chapter Eight

How Kandar kept his word and how they came to Lodge Ascapard.

When, as a child, Kandar had been dressed in his best princely costume and had gone with his father and mother and uncles and aunts and his brother and sister to the white and golden glory of the Temple of Helios, he had understood that his father, Pandin Heliodotus, was in some strange way not easily understood by a child's mind the representative of Helios here on Earth. That had seemed to him a strange thing, for the court necromancer, Quantoch, had openly wielded powers greater than that of the shadowy Helios. Even if a child could not understand those frightening forces, at least he could respect them.

Later, he had understood that power, too, came from well-drilled and disciplined soldiers, archers, charioteers, swordsmen. He had sought to make himself the most proficient in arms in all Akkar. But the powers of the gods had escaped him for many years.

He had read widely, reveling in the old stories, all the colored myths and fables of Fair Akkar, the livelier rollicking yarns of the seacoast and the earthier country wisdom from the hinterlands, beyond Sanghara of the many looms.

He had not, until now, heard of Nga-ereshvigal or of the enchanted Isle of Histiaea.

He was coming to a reluctant comprehension that this world was a vaster place than he had imagined, that Akkar was not all of the world, that beyond the barbarians who hemmed in his homeland stretched other kingdoms and empires. The itch to spur back to Ferranoz possessing him was curiously muted by a newly discovered urge to travel these vaster lands and to joy in the undiscovered country, the thrill of fresh adventures. Discovery—that was the keynote of his life.

They walked, a little footsore, into Grimwald and put up at a comfortable inn, sleeping after Koztivkure had been joyously unsheathed through the hot daytime. That evening, soberly, Kandar faced the unpalatable fact that he must now leave Thurder the Cunning's jade casket where the evil wizard could recover it. That much, he had promised.

He had dreamed badly. Lurid visions of monstrous flying dragons with toad-men wielding serrated swords ten feet long screeching from their leathery backs, tall columns of fire dancing about him, and he, himself, screaming as he tried to break through those living bars of flame. The face of Elthalee swam up through the haze, to be followed by the simpering shallowness of Aylee. Then the nameless escaped temple-prophetess, the nude girl who had run with Krak. Finally Angelena's warm copperskinned face glowed through the nimbus of vanishing horror and he awoke to the feel of her firm body in the crook of his arm.

She smiled at him, lazily, and, shaken by the remembered terrors, he sought sanctuary with her. She responded to his embrace with passionate sincerity. At last, drained, he flopped back in the wide, tumbled bed.

"By the honeyed lips of sweet Vashtilulu the Buxom!" roared a joyous voice in his mind. "That was gorgeous! What a toothsome morsel!"

"Krak!" he yelled, outraged. He jerked up, livid with fury. "Were you—?"

"I was! You surprised me, boy! Your technique needs a little . . . um . . . polishing, but you perform well! I shall enjoy this little honey pot!"

Tosho's sly giggle echoed that sentiment.

Deep shame flooded Kandar. He felt dirtied, ashamed, outraged. Then, some of the responsibility he owed these two poor spirits locked temperamentally in his mind made him see what he owed them.

Angelena lifted on an elbow to look at him with drowning eyes. "Oh, Kandar, you are . . . more than a man!"

He burst out laughing. "You're too right! I'm at least three men—three of us—come here!"

When at last a semblance of sobriety returned, Kandar said, "We need horses, or Dumarests, we have to pay the reckoning here, and we must get to Histiaea—"

She touched her torn pants belt. A brown pouch, locked with a gilt device, opened. She poured bright golden coins over his naked body. The metal struck him cool, like a summer shower of golden dewdrops from an ambrosia tree. "There, lover."

"I can't . . ."

"Don't be tiresome! We travel together. We share." She rose, stretching, her flesh firm and taut. "I'm having a bath. You go down and buy all that is necessary."

He had just reached the courtyard of the inn, conscious of his bedraggled appearance, and was making an arrangement with the landlord, when he saw a dusty brown figure staggering toward them. One look was enough. He ran swiftly forward and caught the man as he dropped.

"Alleyn! You got away! Thank Bright Helios!"

As soon as Alleyn had been found a room and seen to, a local goodwife coming in with hot water and unguents and country medicine, Kandar completed his business. He bought six Dumarests, intending now he had the chance to try this form of transport. A mass of clothing, hampers of food and wine, stores, preceded the important and pleasant task of choosing weapons.

They would set off early next morning. He did not consult Alleyn or Angelena, but bought two sturdy crossbows, both of the type spanned by a rack and pinion, together with a good supply of quarrels. He chose the type feathered with leather rather than with thin wood. The quarrels, driven by the laminated bows, were guaranteed to be lethal at extreme ranges. He found it difficult to buy rapiers, but eventually purchased two and, for himself, a heavier double-edged broadsword, straight and with a simple cross-guarded hilt. The merchant with whom he dealt wished to press all manner of armor on him, scenting easy money; but Kandar contented himself with three bronze helmets with neck flaps and brims, and three leather tunics, partially reinforced with bronze plates, primitive jacks. Some lands had never properly grasped the significant use of steel in weapons, preferring the more easily worked bronze. At that, the armor seemed of excellent workmanship.

Early the next morning, they set off. Alleyn, a toughened old bird, wore his bandages as badges of prowess. Of his three dead companions, after a short word, they did not speak again. Death was a familiar occurrence. The dead were mourned in dignity.

Tosho, apprehensively, said, "I think the border is beyond that little stream." They rode toward the hump-backed bridge. There was no sign of a border guard. "The Kingdom of Taractea exercises powers of overlordship over the next province. Count Naras—he takes his name from the province, Narascum—is a vassal of King Taractacus." The squeaky voice keened alarm. "But this is the border."

"Just what is in the jade casket?"

Krak rumbled, "Wizardry . . ."

Tosho shushed him. "A simulacrum of Thurdur, stuck with bits of his hair and skin and nail-parings. Any enchantment he throws against the possessor of the simulacrum will recoil on his own head. Sympathetic magic, if believed in by the practicers, works."

The Dumarests click-clopped-clicked on. The hump-backed bridge came nearer.

"I'll leave the casket on the bridge," Kandar decided. "If Thurdur is as cunning as he is reputed, he will know."

He felt uneasy about the decision. On the bridge, with the animals' hooves echoing hollowly, he reined in. He took the casket from his belt. He now wore fresh new green trousers and shirt, but the belt was the same old belt from far-off Ferranoz, the belt from which once had swung Skullskelper. Angelena looked across enquiringly.

Kandar felt a stirring in the air. He sensed the beat of unseen powers. His flesh crawled.

He ought to ride on—not like the very devil, but as though the very devil was at his heels. He opened the casket to look at this devil's image.

The casket was empty.

He broke out into a profuse sweat. A drunken roaring washed in his head. He almost fell off the Dumarest.

This—this nothingness—this was what had protected him! But it couldn't have—he saw the answer and knew he had confronted Thurdur the Cunning and Myder with nothing but an unknowing bluff.

He felt ill. His face was as white as green cheese.

"May the slimy black tapeworms of Kragunoth's diseased intestines take the bitch!" boomed Krak's mighty voice.

"She followed her trade to the last!" squeaked Tosho, almost inaudible with the fear that gripped them all.

"Kandar! What is it?" Angelena's voice came as though from a long distance, frightened, raucous; far fainter, though, than the clashing oaths resounding in his head from Krak and Tosho.

As though he had touched a black viper, Kandar slammed the casket shut. It seemed to burn his palm. He shook with the very suddenness of this panic.

At that very moment of horror the monstrous figure of Myder appeared on the bridge, barring their way, flaming and horned and altogether terrible.

Angelena screamed. Alleyn threw up his crossbow.

"Wait!" choked Kandar. "Wait!"

From Myder flowed that unearthly brilliance. The glint of steel mesh, the billowing robes, the horned head, all combined to close down in a ring of terror on the mortals on the bridge.

The honed voice, scalpel sharp, cut across the sunshine.

"My master has waited, petty princeling. He has contained his anger. For he well knows you will honor your word inside the boundaries of the Kingdom of Taractea!"

Upflung in Kandar's hand, the casket's jade abruptly glowed with evil emerald light, pulsing like a lambent heart of stone!

Bravely, Alleyn and Angelena crowded close to Kandar.

"I honor my word!" shouted Kandar, high and hard. "I promised to kill Tosho of the small talents and to return the jade casket to Thurdur the Cunning! Tosho is slain! Here is the casket!" And he flung the glowing throbbing thing to the stones of the bridge.

"Ride!" he screamed at his companions. He thwacked Angelena's Dumarest and jerked the reins of his own. Alleyn whistled a shrill command, and the three beasts flung themselves forward, followed by the three pack animals. In a wild stampede they thundered over the bridge.

Kandar cast a frantic glance back.

The jade casket, blazing its evil emerald brilliance, floated into the air. It rose higher, spinning, turned and was sucked into the greater brilliance of Myder.

The lathe voice keened. "You have kept your word, princeling. My master has the casket. But I do not advise you again to cross his path!"

Kandar shuddered. When he looked back again, Myder had vanished.

"Ride!" snarled Kandar, the fear clogging his mouth and throat. He tried to spit and could not.

"How long, Tosho, how long?" he asked the spirit within his brain.

Tosho's squeak sounded lost. "I do not know!" The warlock of small talents was badly rattled. "In the name of sweet Majus! The casket was empty all the time! A temple-prophetess knows well the devil's arts!"

Riding furiously, urging the bewildered Angelena and Alleyn on, Kandar remembered that wild scramble with the nude girl there outside Tosho's cave, with the dead bodies of the two he now counted his greatest friends lying among the rocks. Her arms and hands, buried in the mass of her auburn hair—he could see it all now. Under cover of that rippling mass she had opened the casket, taken out the image of Thurdur. Then, when his clumsy advances had besotted him enough, she had thrust shrewdly with a knee, leaving him blind with pain, and run off, taking the image with her. How she had fooled him!

The Dumarests sensed danger. They galloped fleetly.

"She was always a cunning wench!" growled Krak. "I found her, abased, and befriended her. She acted according to her lights. But you—Our Kandar—you walked into a danger so great—unprotected! By Crox—it scares me!"

For the rest of that day they rode hard northwards. Kandar would not let them rest. He beat down Alleyn's automatic protests, and Angelena, clearly sensing something amiss with her man, urged them on as fiercely as Kandar himself. They paced the Dumarests, Alleyn whistling encouragement to them, walking at their sides and riding alternately, not daring to unload their stores to change mounts. Evening sidled up on them out of a misty swamp to their right, the sun descending through beaten gold and copper toward a distant ridge of mountains, and still Thurdur the Cunning had not struck in vicious revenge.

"I think," Tosho said with a throb in his voice, "I think that if Thurdur had opened the casket at once and could still dispatch Myder after us, he would have done so before this."

"You mean we've escaped? By the consoling arms of sweet Vashtilulu the Buxom, I hope you're right!"

As the sun at last winked out in sheets of green and rose, a hamlet stood across their path and they could put up their Dumarests and seek shelter and rest. But for the next and succeeding days they rode hard, not questioning the reasons, both Alleyn and Angelena, with that awesome apparition of the blazing figure of Myder driving them on, following Kandar's lead.

On a number of occasions during that wild ride northwards Tosho and Krak disappeared from Kandar's mind. Their spirits vanished, neither he nor they knew where. They returned, as arbitrarily. Very quickly, Kandar grew to love their presence and to feel tense and irritable if they were not with him.

Gradually, too, the fear or vengeance from Thurdur the Cunning receded. Kandar explained to his companions, who rode their Dumarests alongside him and,

89

with a shudder, they realized the narrowness of their escape.

Twice brigands of the wild places attacked them and twice were routed, with bloodstains to be wiped from all the three blades of the companions. During these bouts Krak raged and roared within Kandar, taking his vicarious pleasures. He shared the pleasures of the bed, too, and now Kandar welcomed the long store of erotic knowledge possessed by Krak and—surprisingly—by Tosho. The three prospered in comradeship.

Then, on a morning when the sun beat down fiercely and the grass beside the road grew drooping and yellow, Angelena said: "This day, Kandar, we shall sight my home."

He had never asked her what she had been doing so far south and now, when he mentioned it, her face darkened. "I had been to bury my brother, Alan, slain none would say how, but slain nevertheless. He had been long dead when the news reached us at Lodge Ascapard, and long in the ground when I rode into Gilgal. But he had to be buried according to the rites, in a seemly way, with proper offerings to Bright Gyrane. This I did."

That would explain her sudden changes of mood; grief for her brother mingled with the knowledge that he was long dead, and her task carried out with the dignity death required. With his own allegiance to Helios, he found an unexpectedly awkward friction at this mention of Gyrane. There were many gods, he was finding out, as there were many lands.

They rode on into a land that burned with heat, where the grasses grew thin, where duststorms whirled crazily up out of nowhere. Occasional streams meandered untidily, giving precarious life to lines of trees chopped into the horizons. Flying dots which haunted their trail, did not venture close, but followed them all day.

"Scavengers," grunted Alleyn contemptuously. "Bright Gyrane help a man who breaks a leg here."

They saw vast herds of animals browsing, tails eternally flicking, heads down. Downwind of the humans, the animals reacted at once, galloping away in a heaving sea of rumps and tails.

Now, Kandar understood why these men were hunters.

"The grass will not support even half-domesticated beasts," Angelena told him. "The animals of the wild are tougher, stronger, and breed more freely than any we could pen in. It is a hard life. But this is my home."

Much of her character was explained now.

Then, with a shock wholly out of proportion, he saw the sea.

They had ridden up a slight incline, the dust kicking beneath the Dumarests' hooves, and there, burning beneath the sun, lay the sea.

"How can it be?" marveled Kandar.

Angelena laughed, a little bitterly, resigned to her land. "The coast curves sharply eastwards. But the water does nothing to make this land fertile. Men call that coastline Skeleton Shore."

"The salt leaches everywhere along there," observed Alleyn. "It is bad country."

When at last a lackadaisical creek came into view and the adobe buildings of a hunting lodge, surrounded by living quarters and stables, showed among stunted trees, Kandar was glad to rest. They rode up in a flurry of barking dogs, scuttling chickens, shrieking children and the delighted yelling of brown-faced men and bright-eyed women.

A tall man, whipcord tough, clad in faded brown leathers and wearing a jeweled rapier, engulfed Angelena, lifting her from her steed with accustomed loving strength. His face was a counterpart of Alleyn's, with the added lines of domination and habitual authority. Clearly, in that face, Kandar could see the resemblance to Angelena.

Excitement and movement surrounded them. Then a woman began sobbing over by a sun-baked wall. Alleyn stood there, distressed, helpless. Women's hands pushed him away. He turned, looking dejected. Kandar thought of the forest of Semele and the monkey-ghouls.

But death had to be considered in the light of life; these were here, with their lives to live, even if three men of Ascapard lay rotting in the forest of Semele.

That night there was a great feast, with Kandar as guest of honor. Much home-brewed wine was drunk, many fabulous stories were told, and the young men displayed their prowess. When it was all over and the stars twinkled high, Angelena crept into the room given to Kandar. There was no shame in their love-making, but all the same, by morning she had gone back to her own bedchamber.

Beginning with that second day at Lodge Ascapard, Kandar began planning. Angelena insisted on going with him. Athelstan, dubiously, allowed she was old enough to do as she pleased. Kandar tried to dissuade her.

Laughingly, she referred to the great sword Koztivkure that had excited so much interest among the rapier-wielding hunters. At last, Kandar consented. Alleyn, with fresh hunters at his back, would go also. A boat would be purchased.

"The hunting has been good this season, even though the poachers grow ever bolder," Athelstan told Kandar. "If Angelena wishes to spend her portion in buying a boat from up the coast, and provisioning it, well—" He glanced meaningfully at Kandar and chuckled. "Well, may Bright Gyrane bless her, say I."

"Only for the sake of Ferranoz!" That, swore Kandar, was the only reason. He liked Angelena, surely he did. She was a marvelous bed-partner. But he did not love her, not with the love he knew he could find for a girl one day. But for a man willing to sell his soul to put right the wrong done his city—a wrong he felt he had caused—trading a little on a girl's heart did not come too hard.

Krak and Tosho kept silent on that touchy point.

The days and weeks skipped by with hunting forays and expeditions and the provisioning of the boat. Then, on a morning when the sun glanced off the sea in bright promise, they set sail for the Isle of Histiaea and the wizard Nga-ereshvigal, servant of the Lord of Shadows.

Chapter Nine

Of The Trilogos Damnae.

Helplessly, gripped in the raging torrents of a violent sea tempest, came Kandar of Ferranoz to the Isle of Histiaea.

He stood in the prow of the ship grasping a stayline, peering through drenching sheets of water, feeling the boat rising and falling in gasping sobs of working timbers, the seas a maelstrom of madness about him. Strong-backed oarsmen struggled with blades that bucked and snapped, oars that flew like kindling in the smash of the sea. The wind keened in razored lines of violence, slicing off wave-crests, heeling the boat over so that white water foamed over her lee gunwale. The uproar continued in a blended note of blustering confusion.

As the boat rose and fell and the churned-up seas fell upon him with shattering violence, Kandar shook his head savagely and peered ahead. Was that the loom of land? Were there black cliffs out there?

Then he roared like a king-obi through the storm, booming, raucous, "Land! Land! By Helios, it must be Histiaea!"

Wearily, Alleyn dragged himself along the lifeline to which they were all lashed in running loops. Angelena, to her own anger and violent disapprobation, was by Kandar's orders belowdecks.

"Land, is it, Kandar? Aye, land, right enough—"

A chill dismay gripped Kandar. Was the stout-hearted hunter already beaten by the storm, by the stories seamen had whispered in sleazy ports about Histiaea?

"We'll soon be ashore, and light a fire, Alleyn! Then we'll warm our bones and eat and drink!"

93

"You're right, Kandar, aye, you're right." And Alleyn inched back through the floods of green water to superintend the bailers.

The wind pushed the boat nearer. The sails and masts had long since been unshipped by the storm. They were rudderless and near-oarless; they were floating into the island like a rolling log of wood.

Kandar glanced up. The midday darkness spread a pall of gloom. Water battered his face, and he jerked down, stung by the lash of rain and spray. Ahead lofted the cliffs, sheer black bulwarks towering menacingly up, ominous and hostile.

Like a half-staved-in barrel they drifted into a wide bay walled by the frowning cliffs. Hurled hither and thither by clashing currents and contrary winds they were at last dashed to pieces against a broad foam-laced ledge of rock, black and green with age.

With Angelena firmly clinched in his left arm, with Koztivkure on his back—and with precious little else —Kandar scrambled and clawed his way ashore. A black hole of a cave opened off the ledge, dark and dank and unprepossessing. With bloodied knees and hands, the remaining crewmen crawled out of the sea and huddled in the cave.

"So we've reached the island," panted Alleyn, drawing the back of his hand across his cheek, where blood flowed.

"Now," spat back Angelena with fiery spirit, "we must climb through into the island!" She pointed to the back of the cave. "There is a draught of air. There must be a way!"

"There will be a better chance of dry wood for a fire and fresh water farther inland," said Kandar. He stood up. He smiled at Angelena. "Shall we start?"

They began to climb, in darkness and cold, with the distant booming roar of the wind and sea dying to their rear into a muffled snoring. This was not the way Kandar had envisaged landing on the Isle of Histiaea. Half-drowned, bloodied, faint for want of rest, bedraggled and with only half of the good companions left to him, no, this was not to his liking at all.

At last, sick of the dark winding tunnels beneath the

cliffs, they clawed their way up and out onto a gaunt cleft between mountains. Giant white birds with bright intelligent eyes circled them, cawing menacingly.

"A lost tomb, ruined and forgotten!" mumbled Alleyn.

The brooding menace of the hills ringed them in.

"We'll find it!" cried Angelena, her coppery face alive and vibrant, her body braced. "By Bright Gyrane, we will find it!"

At that moment, if at no other, Kandar could have loved her.

They marched inland, twoscore men and a girl, bruising their feet on the unyielding rocks, climbing over the high saddle of the mountains and so descending on the other side into the jungle wilderness of the interior.

They hacked their way a little distance into the jungle, slashing at trailing lianas and groping half-sentient fronds, avoiding giant flowers that sought for them with blind hungrily sucking cups, until they reached a stream. Here, as night fell with a pandemonium of shrieks and calls from the nighted jungle about them, they set a fire and rested.

With what food they had with them heated and eaten, with their thirsts quenched, with a watch set and the others curled up for sleep, Kandar felt a tiny returning flicker of confidence. Tomorrow—tomorrow they would see.

The storm had died out on the morrow. The sun burned down. Vapors rose from the jungle. A brooding breath of miasmic horror seemed to enwrap the men struggling through the island's heart. Everyone sensed that eerie feeling, as though invisible eyes watched them. They came at last to the mountains ringing the northern and western section of the island. They had found no signs of intelligence, no life apart from the swarming terrors of the jungle.

Three black dots, high, flew in a straight line out of the westward. They reached a tall double-peak directly to the front of the halted party. At a point exactly halfway between the gaunt peaks the flying dots circled once, then dived straight down. They vanished behind the upflung violence of the jungle.

Alleyn shuddered. "Evil!" he said, his tanned face an unhealthy color. "I can sense it—they mean us harm!"

Angelena tried to rally him. But she, too, like them all,

95

could feel the uneasy pressures, the sensation of suffocating horror, holding this lost island in its shadowy grip.

Again Kandar cursed the emptiness inside his mind, the black gulf that spawned there like a suppurating nightmare when Krak and Tosho were not with him. He needed their help and advice now—the cunning practicality of Tosho and the booming recklessness of Krak. Silently, the party moved on through the flaunting colors of the jungle.

In the succeeding ten days they covered the island from all points of the compass and found nothing. Oh, they stumbled across bones, skeletons of men long rotted into the jungle floor, their rusted weapons and equipment at their sides, but of any clue to the tomb they found no sign. The hunters with professional skill brought down birds and animals for good food; they drank water from the streams; they ate fruit. At last, forcing himself to the point, Kandar told the others, "We must climb to that high saddle, the place between those peaks where the flying things landed."

Frightened faces met his. Angelena laid her slender but firm hand on her rapier hilt. Alleyn looked sullen.

"Most of you will remain below." Kandar knew enough to know that pressed men would be useless. "I will take six volunteers." He had his eye on a full-bearded rascal called Althun—nearly all the people of Ascapard had names beginning with the letter "A"—a man who spoke seldom, and when he did, with an oath and to the point.

Althun nodded savagely. "I'd like to sink my steel into the guts of someone, by Weglac!"

Four other tough, cynical, cursing men stepped forward, one hunter and three seamen. Kandar rejected one seaman; the man was so strung up he would have collapsed like a pricked balloon at the first moment of danger.

Angelena stepped out with them.

Kandar stopped.

"No," he said harshly. "No, my lady."

She stared at him, her face flushed, her hair tumbled, and her breasts heaving. "Yes," she said stubbornly. "Yes, my prince! For I will not be parted from you."

Everyone took it for granted that both the tomb they sought and the evil that breathed over this island would be found between those two gaunt peaks.

"Alleyn!"

The hunter stepped forward, his face ashamed.

"Take care of your mistress! She will remain down here with you. If I am not back before tomorrow night, well . . ."

"We will mourn you as is befitting," said the hunter, taking Angelena's arm. "My lady—"

She broke free and flung herself into Kandar's arms, pressing against him, kissing him, sobbing, blindly seeking to take from him an assurance he could hardly give.

"Kandar!"

He put her back. He smiled for a moment on her, knowing her good; then he turned and with a hitch to his sword swung off along the trail. His four men followed, cursing.

They climbed for the rest of the day, pausing only to eat their provisions, until at nightfall they came to a scree leading precariously up to a ridge. After a scramble they reached the ridge and inched along the ledge. Cautiously, Kandar had led them around and higher so that they could look down into the space between the peaks.

They saw a shallow bowl among the rocks, with strange and ominous monoliths standing in a circle. A central stone, darkly stained, indicated the nature of the ceremonies carried out there.

Creatures thronged the open space. As they watched, more arrived, flying down the wind, alighting in a great flapping of ebon wings.

"By Weglac!" grunted Althun. He gripped his sword, and his stained teeth showed in a rictus of a grin. "A coven!"

Strange and eerie and repellent were the creatures within the circle of stones. Kandar saw worm-shapes, dragon-shapes, bat-shapes, manticores of frightful appearance, and naked women, dancing, their upflung arms and waving hair striking a chill into the watchers.

On an ebony throne sat the chief, presiding over the abominable rites. Horned, cloaked in darkness, with eyes that seemed lit with a light of their own, ruby-red, feral, evil, he brooded over that blasphemous assembly.

For men from a land who did not own to sorcerers, the men with him knew well enough when to be afraid.

97

"Sardan!" rose the chant from below. "All hail to the Lord of Shadows, to Sardan, Prince of Darkness."

To remain where they were smacked of imbecility. At any moment a baleful gleaming eye could be raised, could see them, could bring the screeching rout down upon them. All the swords in Akkar would not suffice at that moment of supreme horror.

"Oh, for Quantoch!" groaned Kandar in that terrible agony of frustration when he knew himself impotent to carry on. He began to edge back.

The light of torches splashed lurid colors on the rocks. Althun, moving clumsily, dislodged a stone. It rumbled away below, picked up others, started a slide down the scree.

The five men halted in a stasis of terror.

A movement began within the circle of stones—upward. Black wings thrashed. Bat-shapes rose out of the torchlight.

One of the men with Kandar began to giggle helplessly. Kandar slapped his face, hard.

Upslope, the dark slashes of cracks in the rock showed the chance of shelter. Kandar gestured and began to climb. The others followed, swearing heavily, sweating with fear.

They reached the cracks and began to force themselves into the crevices. A sword scabbard clashed. Kandar struggled through. The others, separately, thrust through the cracks, which revealed themselves as the teeth-like entrances to a low, wide, cave, dark and smelling of fungus.

Turning at once, Kandar peered out.

Hideous shapes flapped across his line of vision.

He swallowed and felt the dryness of his mouth. For a long time those dread shapes patrolled.

Althun whispered in his ear, breathing stertorously.

"The cave goes on down. It might lead us back to the jungle, like the caves we came up through from the sea—"

At once Kandar nodded. "Right. Lead on, Althun."

In a single line, after the first few steps with Kandar leading, they crept on through the darkness. A straggle of luminous fungi gave sufficient light to see the loom of darkness and the winding course of the cave, which trended ever downwards.

After some time Kandar became convinced the cave was leading them back beneath the bowl of rock and the upright stones, and not toward the jungle. He did not reveal his thoughts. This way, at least, they were under cover, and he had no wish to scare these men more than they were already.

A stream began to plash beside them; as they crept on, it broadened until they were walking along a ledge above a rushing torrent. Light grew. The fungi thickened and clumped and in the dim radiance Kandar saw an arched opening directly ahead. They had to go on through it. There was no other way.

He drew his sword, the straight broadsword he had bought in Grimwald so long ago. With the blade naked in his hand he edged along toward the archway.

Strong in him was the fearful idea that if he tried to employ sorcery now, the horned demon above, Sardan, Lord of Shadows, would instantly know—would know and would dispatch his horde of familiars to blast the puny mortals into a pit from which they would never return.

Through the archway a tumbled mass of ruined masonry met his gaze. Fallen columns, shattered pillars, piles of scattered roofing timbers, rotten and inhabited by scuttling beetles, and algae-covered heaps of broken bricks and mutilated marbles lay strewn everywhere. It looked as though a proud building had been blasted and torn down by an explosion of supernal violence.

But a fierce exultation blazed up in Kandar.

"The tomb!" he cried. "The lost tomb of Ngareshvigal!"

"It must be," growled Althun. "By Weglac! I'm scared!"

The others crowded through.

Directly above their heads, and separated by layers of rock of an unknown thickness, cavorted the bestial familiars of Sardan at their blasphemous rites. Kandor did not want to inquire too closely who might be stretched face-up on that stained stone and whose blood might drain from a slit throat to mingle with those other age-old stains. He moved on, looking eagerly about him.

"A book!" he said in a hard, tense voice. "A great volume bound in dragonskin. It must be here! It must be!"

99

Now absolutely convinced that he must find *The Umbre Testament,* he scrabbled among the ruins of the fallen temple, urging the others on, overturning piles of masonry, digging in heaps of brick dust, clawing rotten timbers away in a smoking powder of brown chips and scuttling beetles.

As he knew he must, so he found it.

In what must have been the diametrically central point of the temple he kicked the yellowed skull and powdery bones of a skeleton long dead. Around the vertebrae a golden chain's links winked back an unsullied fire in the fungus illumination. At the end of the chain—at the end, unharmed, dusty but intact, lay a great dragonskin-bound volume. His heart gave a huge leap. His pulses hammered. Hardly daring to believe, he bent, snapped the chain in one savage burst of energy, and lifted the book.

"Now thanks be to Great Helios!" he breathed, exalted. He felt strongly the presence of the spirit of the omnipotent Heliodotus, and as much a thanksgiving gesture as a charm against the fiends leaping and cavorting above him, he signed the secret sign in the air before him, the sign that his father, Pandin Heliodotus, would use in blessing.

Dust slithered thickly from the tattered pages. This had been an ancient tome when Nga-ereshvigal had acquired it. The dragonskin binding looked splotched, unhealthy.

"He served a foul master," whispered Kandar. "And although he lies here in death, his bones shattered and abandoned, his master and his familiars carry on their own old blasphemous rites above."

"We are in mortal peril," said Althun, thickly. His broad face sheened with sweat; drops caught the dim illumination and sparkled in his beard. "By Weglac! This place is evil!"

Summoning up all his mental strength, Kandar called into the blank emptiness that dwelt in his skull where should be his two companions, Krak and Tosho, he called on them for help. Only silence and the rushing beat of his own blood answered.

One of the seamen called to Althun, his voice hoarse and greedy.

"Here, Althun! You were right!" He held up a hand, and jewels flamed in a stream. "See!"

Spilled from shattered oaken chests, an emperor's fortune lay strewn amongst the ruins.

The four men with Kandar forgot by some subtle mental alchemy their fears. Like gray wolflings they pounced on the gold and jewels. Now Kandar understood why they had volunteered. They must have heard the story that Angelena had heard, a story that contained treasure.

Well, they had found their treasure. Whether they would live to spend it in whoring and drinking and living or not, Kandar for one would not have liked to risk the odds. And their lives were as precariously balanced as his own. He hitched up his sword, clasped the precious volume of arcane lore to him, and said roughly, "Gather up what baubles you can. We cannot abide here. We must leave now!"

Each man there had found the treasure he sought, yet only Kandar was ready to leave now. The others scooped up the gems and the gold, stuffing their clothes with them, laughing, oblivious to the menace that only a moment ago had been scourging them with whips of fear.

"Come!" commanded Kandar, angry and concerned at the delay. He could not allow himself to break down now.

With a half-laughable hang-over of his princely days he felt he owed these men some loyalty. He went over to Althun and hoisted him up with a single twist of one powerful arm. Althun's face, alight with greed, looked up blindly.

"We must get away!" Kandar said harshly. "Have you forgotten what is above us?"

"The treasure!" Althun said thickly, struggling to break free. Kandar shook him.

Another man groped after a leather satchel of emeralds. The leather was rotten, split. The gems poured out.

"Put them in this bag," grunted his fellow.

"That leather is as rotten as this. For safety we shall split them between us. Hey—Althun—hurry!"

Kandar let Althun go. The big bearded man fell to his knees and began stuffing emeralds into his tunic front.

A sickness possessed these men. Kandar could sympathize, could not condemn. Tosho had told him more of the plight of the poor than anything he had ever learned as a Prince of Akkar had done. Now he gripped the book under his arm, his sword still back in its scabbard, the great blade of Koztivkure dangling on his back. He must find a better light than this to read the book by.

One last time—and then again—he pleaded with the riches-crazed men. Then he left them and began to work his way back through the ruins. He reached a spot where a coalescing flood of light from massed fungi promised illumination enough. Here he trod on the broken bones of skeletons, men who had come seeking the treasure and had found only death for their pains. Kandar of Ferranoz had no time for shuddery sympathy. Feeling the blood pounding in his veins, feeling the trembling in his muscles, he opened *The Umbre Testament*.

A single blow with his sword smashed the golden lock that kept the last section secret.

Again he thought of the two previous occasions when he had pored over a great tome of thaumaturgical lore. This time the light poured weakly from glowing fungi, deep beneath the ground under the rocks where a ghastly coven met in blasphemous rites. He saw once again the old familiar spells, of Kholokova and Sassilinja, of retaining the spirit of a man slain in battle—oh, Krak and Tosho, how he needed them now!—and the others, half of which he had read on the Plain of Steeds and the balance skipped through in Thurdur the Cunning's ghastly chamber of horrors.

The parchment here must have been flayed virgins' skins, but the color was darker, deeper, as though girls from a hotter clime had been used. He thought when he turned the page from Sassilinja that the writing at the top of the next page had been obliterated. Then he saw that a spell began a third of the way from the bottom of the page. He recalled that Thurdur's *Ochre Scroll* had possessed in the space before Kholokova a spell—which he had read through in desperate haste—written across the center of the page. That spell had had neither beginning nor end. This spell in the *Testament* had no beginning, but it did own to an end.

Kandar began to see, or hoped, frantically, that he could see. Under his hand lay a third of a spell. The second part was that fragment in the *Scroll*. Then . . . ?

"By Dangorn!" he whispered fiercely. "The first part of

102

the spell must have been in Quantoch's *Thaumalogicon!*"

But the book of sorcery had been slashed diagonally in two by a raking wolfling sword!

Convinced now that for safety the dread spell to summon the greater intelligences had been split into three by the compiler of *The Trilogos Damnae,* Kandar turned quickly to the end paper for confirmation. The bloody skull with the lily clenched in its gappy teeth had been the imprimatur here, also. He felt sure. The unknown sorcerer who had compiled these books—and just how many copies he had issued Kandar had no way of knowing—had been well aware of the dread power of the knowledge he had committed to writing.

The Thaumalogicon, the book of spells, promised what was to come, and in *The Ochre Scroll* that information was carried on, to come to a conclusion in *The Umbre Testament.* For to what did this tome testify, if not to the consummation of the enchantment and spell? And as the color deepened, through that ochreous yellow to this smoky dark umbre, so the power and knowledge of that power grew.

And—the three volumes together—why should they be called *The Trilogy of the Damned* if not because this consummated spell would condemn to eternal damnation the soul of the men desperate enough to call on the great spirits? He had two thirds of the spell that would call the greater intelligences to his aid and the aid of ensorcelled Ferranoz.

The remaining third, the first third, had been written in the book which had been slashed in half. He sweated, then. He felt a physical pain in his guts. Suppose . . . !

He refused to admit that dread possiblity.

He began to cast back in his mind to *The Thaumalogicon.*

A frightful shriek shattered the still air of the entombed ruins.

Kandar stared up, for a moment his eyes still focused back in time upon that book there on the Plain of Steeds.

A ghastly rout poured into the ruins. Flaring torches, some the Hand of Glory, spilled a lurid light over the scene. Shapes flowed. Dark wings clashed against rock. Dust puffed. Horned, hooded, web-footed, spined and armor-plated, the horrors flooded across Althun and his comrades.

Gold and gems ran to sparkle emptily in the debris.

The whole specter crew had burst down upon them!

He snatched out his sword and a bolt of purple fire cracked from a scaled nightmare and slewed the blade from his hand in a tingle of excruciating pain.

Flame bit into his side.

As Thurdur's jade casket had glowed, so now *The Umbre Testament* glowed and boiled with an evil radiance.

"By Helios!" shouted Kandar, defiant. He threw the scorching book from him. It lay on a shattered marble slab and burned, and yet was not consumed.

He could not remember the beginning of the only spell in all the world that could aid him now.

He stood erect, proud, not owning his fear, sweating and dry-throated, burning-eyed, feeling the tangible presence of evil.

Stumblingly, frantically, his brain sought through the slashed leaves of *The Thaumalogicon* for the beginning of the incantation.

The coven closed on him.

Horned shapes bore down on him. Scaled legs and arms struck him. Claws ripped his tunic, his body. His blood flowed in jagged slashes of pain.

For a few moments he struck out wildly; then the final blow smashed against his head, and he slumped, and the blackness took him like a booming geyser of night.

Chapter Ten

Of Red Hair and of Silver Hair and how Vrinda of the Nimble Feet, my Lady of the Scaled Cloud, commanded the great sword Koztivkure.

He lay on the stone block, bound with thongs plaited from flayed human skin, stretched out with his head dangling and his throat a taut bar upturned to the stars.

Around him circled widdershins the throng of awesome figures.

Sardan, the Lord of Shadows, the Prince of Darkness, sat on his throne and glowered down with his eyes of hellfire.

"By the corrupt and worm-eaten heart of Kragunoth! You get yourself into some mighty fine fixes, Our Kandar!"

"By the light of sweet Majus we are all likely to be killed now!"

The leap of pure joy at his comrades' return overwhelmed the fears in Kandar. Surely, now, with these two good companions in his mind he could not die!

The ritual dance continued. Many of the dancers gyrated back-to-back. Others leaped and cavorted in maniacal bounds. Drums beat. The torchlight flared in demoniac splashes and splodges of color.

To Kandar everything appeared upside-down. He lay feeling the blood sluggishly pounding in his head, his body numb, and yet his mind was active and alive and pulsing with the renewed determination to remember the beginning of the incantation of power.

Krak grunted like a wounded Jagardu of the Langaan Hills.

"Can't you get a hand free? By the bounteous bottom of sweet Vashtilulu the Buxom! If I could but swing Koztivkure at these fiends!"

"It is evil magic, evil," squeaked Tosho.

Koztivkure gleamed in a magnificent flash of naked steel in the clawed hand of Sardan. The great sword rose as though in blasphemous blessing of the assembly.

When Krak saw that, his mental blast shredded Kandar's nerves.

"By Crox! I'll disembowel the foul beast! Koztivkure!"

"Stop yammering, you two!" snarled Kandar. "Pleased as I am that you have returned, I must try to remember!"

He told them what he must know.

"It is our only chance!" he finished.

They picked up at once the desperate fears lurking in his mind, battened down by his own pride and by his dominating sense of urgency. They quieted.

Since beginning this quest he had been forced to use magic that was imprecise, chancy, often resulting in opposite effects from those he wished to contrive. Many times, believing in the lights of science, he had been forced to use his sword to overcome opposition. But now—lying spread-eagled for sacrifice on this blood-stained block —he knew without doubt he must summon all his own powers to aid him and to dredge from his mind the memory of the spells, the three parts of the dread spell, that would summon to him the greater intelligences he had sought for so long.

Already he had mentally thumbed through the pages of *The Thaumalogicon* and isolated out the section that he felt must contain the spell's beginning. Now he understood what Thurdur the Cunning had said when he had indicated that although the other spells were the same in both books, their order was different. Thurdur's cunning had balked Kandar from a quicker understanding of what he sought, and now he felt completely free of indebtedness to the evil wizard.

A woman's figure floated apparently upside-down before his straining eyes. Gossamer clad, floating drapes, she twirled before him like a neophyte before the altar. He saw her massy auburn hair, he saw her face, the face he

106

had last seen as she mocked his pain, running fleetly into the night with the contents of Thurdur's jade casket.

"Bitch!" came Krak the Mighty's muted roar.

"She means us mischief this time; she means to finish us off!" squeaked Tosho.

The girl was obviously perfectly at home in her surroundings. Kandar realized, through the horror of the moment, amid the shrieks of the manticores and the flapping of wings, the stamping of cloven hooves and the scraping of claws, that she sang a trilling, spine-chilling ancient song of evil lore and diabolical passion.

In her hands and held between her breasts, she carried a long and slender knife, a dagger blade with wide winged quillons, richly jeweled. Light splintered from the point.

"That's for your throat, by Crox!"

The girl swung her body rhythmically, working herself into a receptive frenzy when she would fling herself upon the supine figure of Kandar.

What was the wording on that page? He struggled to clear his mind of shadows, to hark back to the Plain of Steeds, once again to focus clearly the ripped pages of *The Thaumalogicon*. He had, surely, glanced through the locked last section of the book before it had been slashed? Yes—yes, he had. Kholokova and Sassilinja. They were the key. The second third of the enchantment in the *Scroll* came just before Kholokova, the last third in the *Testament* after Sassilinja. Where, then, would Quantoch's great book hold its secret? Where? The question dinned into his mind, like jungle drums, insistent, maddening.

The nameless girl who was a temple-prophetess swirled in her abandoned dance before him, her white limbs gleaming in torchlight, her massy red hair shot through with gleams of gold. She would with savage lust satisfy her cravings before she slit his throat with that jeweled dagger. He felt the night wind cool on his feverish skin.

"Temple dancer?" roared Krak, unable to contain himself. "By the disgusting gout-swollen left foot of Kragunoth, she's a temple-prostitute! And she'll have you, Our Kandar, she'll have you like a female spider!"

A shudder of dread shivered over Kandar. He knew the stories. "How can I think, with you roaring and raging?" he snapped with sizzling anger.

"Keep quiet, dear Krak, for the sake of your sweet Vashtilulu," pleaded Tosho of the small talents.

Now the rout swung in increasing abandon. Light and shadow alternately flickering, the wild screams of the dancers, the waving of arms and wings and horns, the blowing of trumpets and the beating of drums—all merged into a pandemonium of hypnotic possession.

Then Sardan, Lord of Shadows, rose from his throne and began to speak.

The language rolled sonorously in a tongue completely unknown to Kandar. He guessed sickly it must be the native language of the nameless temple-prophetess. The grand master of the revels descended from his throne, joined the dance, gyrated and swung, moved his body obscenely, laughing, his eyes pits of feral flame.

A surge of arctic hysteria gripped the celebrants so that they all, every single one, moved in unison with Sardan, mimicking his actions and repeating his words.

Closer and closer moved Sardan to the central block.

Suddenly, on a discordant clashing of gongs, cracking through the chanted ritual like a sword slicing through flesh everything ceased. Sardan hung over Kandar. Slowly, he pointed at the auburn-haired girl. She rose, like a snake uncoiling, lifted herself up, shedding the last of her veils. She gyrated her hips. She was lost in the penultimate stages of hypnosis and possession, her eyes flaming on Kandar, her body sheathed in the allure induced by drugs and ritual dancing and abandon.

Women knelt by her, began to anoint her body with oil.

With a shocking repugnance of his own flesh, Kandar felt fingers at work on him, oiling him, long sliding strokes of cunning hands working the magic oil into every part of him, massaging, kneading, making him supple for the role he must play before his death.

The girl lifted herself astride Kandar. He could barely see her face, alight, entranced, enraptured, caught by the diabolism of her abandon to everything but what must happen. She began to sink down onto Kandar, her eyes wide, her lips open, her arms quivering to clasp him.

"By Crox!" whispered Krak. "She'll suck us dry!"

"Think, Our Kandar, in the name of sweet Majus! Remember!"

Kandar could feel the touch of the girl. This he had sought outside Tosho's cave, and he had been crudely rebuffed. Now, he would consummate those bumpkin desires and end them with his death. He struggled, throwing his bound body from side to side, and two crones by his body, giggling, mumbling, vicariously taking their pleasure from the oiled body of the girl, lashed him with whips so that he subsided with a groan. Blood oozed to mingle with the oil.

"Think, Our Kandar! Remember!"

A great book, a dragonskin-bound tome of thaumaturgical lore . . .

"Helios aid me now!" groaned Kandar. Like a bloated spider the girl's body sank down on him.

Kholokova and Sassilinja . . . Retaining the spirit of a man slain in battle . . . Thothak and Mumulak . . . the puissant power of Dangorn . . . Bits of spells clashed and jumbled in his mind. Now he could so easily understand why Quantoch had not cast back an enchantment at the gray wolflings when they had pursued the chariot fleeing across the Plain of Steeds. Of the Caul of Preservation . . . Of the crystal bridge high above the earth . . . Withering of a foeman's right arm . . . Kholokova . . . It had to be, it must be, there could be no other answer . . . .

"Kholokova! Sassilinja!" Kandar cried the names in a gusty darkness of the spirit. The girl's touch revolted him and yet his body like a traitorous minion responded voluptuously. "I call on the omnipotent powers of Kholokova and of Sassilinja!" He repeated the incantation and then went straight on into the second part taken from the *Scroll*. This must be the answer. It must be. The girl was lowering her body forward so that her arms could wrap around his head. He caught a lancing glimpse of the dagger in her hand, the jewels flaming wickedly. Forcing the words out, he cried with a sharp and ejaculatory access of passion, shrieking the last third of the spell taken from the *Testament*. It was done. Limpness overcame him.

He felt drained, dry, emptied.

For a long suspended moment the earth seemed to halt in its progression among the celestial spheres. All noise seemed to attenuate and thin. The dagger held in the clutching hand of the witch-girl touched his throat like the kiss of a viper. He felt its sting.

Then the dagger jerked. Like a live thing it twisted. It glowed! Sparks of golden radiance shot from it.

With a shriek of sobered maniacal terror the girl cast the burning, unconsumed dagger from her.

She shrieked again. Kandar felt her oiled body twisting against him as a great gleaming fish writhes in the net. He exerted all his strength. He burst the bonds of flayed human skin. He broke them with a sundering snap. The girl fell all in a disheveled heap beside the block of sacrifice.

Kandar fell off, rolling over, feeling the rock cool against his oiled body. He crouched and looked up.

What he saw chilled, awed, and elevated him. For a moment he thought he had unlocked the pits of a hell even these deluded people, even Sardan, Prince of Darkness, held beyond their knowledge.

A giant dragon-shape flew down with a slow pinion beat to alight in the rocky bowl. Spined and horned, plated with scales, gleaming gold and silver in liquid runnels of torchlight, the gigantic flying dragon stretched scarlet-clawed talons to scrape rock. Rock crumbled to powdery dust beneath the clutch of those talons. The ring of the coven held positon in a stasis of terror. They were faced with a power greater than the sum of theirs, a power that shocked them into a numbness of spirit vastly debilitating to their proper sense of their own evil importance. Sardan cowered back on his ebony throne, one dark wing covering his face and only the chinks of his crimson eyes glaring.

After that first agonized look, Kandar looked again. The picture sorted itself out. Astride the neck of the dragon, a neck that extended full fifty feet, sat a girl.

She was plump. Her capacious thighs gleamed in a white round of flesh. Her breasts were full and elastic, the nipples covered with glittering stars of jewelry, and gems sparkled in looped and coiled arabesques about her voluptuous body. A necklace scintillated around her neck that like a proud column supported a small head tilted slightly to one side with a poise of absolute arrogance. And her hair! All of spun silver, it glinted and shone and waved like a vast halo, studded with gold and scarlet gems, sparkling, rippling, a silver cloud of gorgeousness.

More than a girl, she was a woman, poised and regal. Her scarlet mouth opened in a wide smile, inviting and commanding. Her green eyes slanted beneath angled brows where kohl enhanced their bright gleaming symmetry. Shapely and radiant appeared this woman. Golden ankle-bells tinkled with a soft melody in the absolute stillness she brought with her. Her face in its graceful perfection bestowed the charm and favor of absolute understanding.

And yet—and yet beneath that fair exterior plainly to be seen and felt as a radiating force, the still firm center of womanliness, of femaleness, alive and as vibrant as the earth-mother herself, conveyed the immediate sense of compassion and love.

Kandar heard Krak's awed whisper.

"By all the gods that ever were! It is sweet Vashtilulu herself!"

The auburn-haired temple-prophetess crouched in a miserable white ball beside the sacrificial block. Now her puppy-like whimpering sobbed into the silence as an affront.

Compared with the matriarch astride the dragon, she appeared a gutter-urchin of contemptible nothingness.

"These foolish revels will stop at once!" chimed the golden bell-voice from the woman. "Disperse! Go your ways. I understand your hearts and sorrow for you. But the words of power have been spoken. Begone!"

Ensued a rustling, hopping, flapping rout. Dark shapes scuttled. Ebony wings flapped. In a diabolic travesty of departure the coven took wing to vanish with screams and whinings and hootings of fear beyond the confines of the rocks.

The dragon's head lowered. Round liquid eyes in vast orbits regarded Kandar. The head of the dragon was round, high-domed, with savage wedge-shaped jaws set with many rows of cutting, slashing, chewing teeth. Yet the whole aspect of the dragon's head was of amiable docility.

"Stay, winged wonder of the sun," crooned the woman Krak thought must be Vashtilulu.

She alighted. The dragon folded his wings in a sibilant

111

clashing. His claws scraped the rock and were silent. Like a basilisk he stood, motionless.

Kandar held his breath.

He trembled at what he had summoned up.

The golden voice chimed again.

"You have summoned the paramount powers. What would you with them, mortal man, knowing your soul forfeit?"

Kandar tried to speak. He swallowed bile. He opened his mouth, and no sounds came.

In that moment of anticipatory terror and hope a single line of a poem he had not heard for years lodged in his mind.

"Lay the bloodied head in the dust of Earth, thy mother."

He understood now what that poem had been saying.

"Yes!" he said, strongly, chewing the word out of a gravel-dry mouth. "Yes, I will sell my soul so that the greater powers you serve shall aid my city of ensorcelled Ferranoz!"

Her eyes melted on him. All the desires for women he had ever felt seemed now to coalesce and fuse and become a single thrust of purest agony. For this woman men would do more than die.

"Ferranoz?" Her chiming voice lilted over the syllables. Her ankle-bells counterpointed the rhythm.

"I know the fair land of Akkar and have often been welcome there. It is the women, too, of that land who most often entreat my aid, for I assuage the birth pain. But you have called on those whom I serve. It is their aid you seek. They will demand not only your soul, but proof that you are worthy to be aided!"

"What proof I can give, that I will give!" Kandar stood up now. He stared at this lush woman frankly. Drained by the auburn-haired temple-prophetess, he yet felt the immediate stir of his interest. "My city of Dreaming Ferranoz lies under the ensorcellment of two interlocking enchantments—"

She nodded with regal condescension.

"We are aware. We mislike the depraved powers that called forth the wolfling horde of the Garfane and hurled them against a mortal city for sport."

"For sport!" echoed Kandar, aghast and somehow defiled by his own impotence.

"By the diseased left testicle of Kragunoth!" growled Krak.

"I am sure, now," squeaked Tosho. "This is the immortal woman Vrinda of the Nimble Feet."

"Nonsense!" rumbled Krak. "She's Vashtilulu."

"She has many names, dear Krak." Tosho knew what he was talking about. "The Lady of the Scaled Cloud; Umiris of the Winged Feet; Vrinda Beloved of gods and men. For, and mark me well, Our Kandar, these powers you have conjured up, vast and all-encompassing though they be and far greater in their lordliness than anything I, of the small talents, might attempt, still remember—they are not gods! Immortals, perhaps; men, possibly; but gods—no!"

"They are mighty powerful," breathed Krak, more subdued than Kandar had ever known him, even when he'd slain him. "Strange and weird and terrible!"

"For sport!" said Kandar, still feeling sick.

The woman's white flesh gleamed in the guttering torchlight; her jewelry sparkled and flashed about her body; the light reflected in twin lambent spots from the eyes of the gigantic winged flying dragon. She smiled sweetly.

"For sport. If you prove yourself, the higher powers will aid you. I promise it—I, Felice Estorcis of the Silver Hair! I promise it on the name of Thorblane here, my faithful steed, Thorblane of the fanged mouth and clawed talons."

Kandar said harshly, "I trust you to keep your word, O Vrinda of the Nimble Feet."

She smiled again, more widely, knowingly.

"You flatter me by knowing one of my names, mortal. I have many, in many lands. One must remember names if one aspires to be an immortal."

"I aspire to save my city."

Vrinda of the Nimble Feet pointed to the foot of Sardan's ebon and abandoned throne. There, like a splinter of flame, lay the great sword Koztivkure.

"Take your sword, mortal. You will have need of it."

"By all the glories before my eyes of sweet Vashtilulu

113

the Buxom!" raged Krak. "Koztivkure is too great a weapon for you to swing!"

"May the strength of sweet Majus be with you and sustain you now, Our Kandar!"

He took up the sword. The weight, although finely balanced, was indeed too great for even his superb strength to wield for long in deadly combat. For a short time he could do murderous damage with this great sword. Then he would tire and his mucles sag, and his enemies would cut him down.

His hand fell to his naked thigh. Skullskelper. Well. Even his good Akkarian leather belt was gone now.

A stir as of invisible wings through the sky lifted his hair. The breeze rustled Vrinda's glory of silver hair. She looked up, smiling, and her arms lifted. The torchlight dimmed as a greater radiance formed. A celestial singing drifted down from above, golden and silver voices muted and commingling with gold and silver instruments. Yet, through the lush strains, a harsher, ominous menacing note pulsed. There were those among the paramount intelligences who displayed reluctance to aid ensorcelled Ferranoz.

Kandar gripped Koztivkure. "I am ready!" he shouted. The challenge whipped into the glowing air, torn from his lips by the blast of wind. Thorblane, the winged wonder of the sun, came to life, bent, seized Kandar around the waist.

He felt those razor-sharp teeth gripping him with a retriever's soft touch. The long sinuous neck swung him dizzily up. He found himself sitting on the jeweled and padded saddle to the rear of Vrinda of the Opulent Charms. She laughed. The sound carried a reckless triumphant clarion call through the bluster of wind.

"Up! Up, Thorblane, my winged wonder! Far across the unlit seas carry us. To the land of Akkar and the ensorcelled city of Ferranoz!"

"But!" gasped Kandar of Ferranoz.

He thought of Angelena, of the others, there on the Isle of Histiaea. But the great wings flapped and bruised the air as the scaled body rose with a clash and scrape against the rocks. The whip tail lashed. Up they rose into the air. Up and up, beating at superhuman speed through the nighted levels, onward and ever onward to the south and east bore Thorblane, the winged wonder of the sun.

Perched on his back, Vrinda of the Silver Hair and Kandar of Ferranoz hurtled toward the city for which he had bargained his soul.

Chapter Eleven

In which the Annals of Akkar record a mighty day of sorcery and of swords.

As naked as the great brand he gripped in his fist, Kandar of Ferranoz, Lion of Akkar, last scion of the Imperial house of Heliodotus, rode down the wind astride the scaled neck of Thorblane, winged wonder of the sun, urged on by Vrinda of the Silver Hair.

Across the dark seas they flew.

He was leaving Angelena and all that new life of Lodge Ascapard. Once more he was hurtling toward his own ensorcelled city where flame and smoke burned and rolled without movement, held in a stasis of enchantment.

"You hold yourself responsible for the doom that fell upon Fair Ferranoz," said Vrinda of the jeweled arms. Through the bluster of the wind her voice chimed like a great brazen bell.

"Yes!" shouted back Kandar. "For I played with my scientific toys with Quarmeln; and Quantoch, his twin brother and the court necromancer—the only man who could have saved the city—had left Doomed Ferranoz to seek me out and reason with me. Had I not done so, had Quantoch been within the city at the first moment of the attack, then—then . . ."

"And you have sold your soul to the greater powers to redeem your city, Kandar of Ferranoz!"

"I have. Willingly! Gladly!"

"I think those whom I serve will not look upon you unkindly, nor without pity, Lion of Akkar."

Kandar's lean arms were clasped about the lushness of Vrinda of the Opulent Charms. He felt the warmth of her flesh beneath his left hand, the great sword Koztivkure gripped in his right. She radiated heat like a copper gong suspended in the sunshine. Kandar felt all his manhood rise to her nearness, and he resolved that if he must lose his life in the battles to come, then he would fight the better for this moment of nearness.

Through the darkness and the wild whirling wastes of the sky they flew. Thorblane's mighty pinions maintained a slow steady threshing of the air. No stars glittered in the sky, no moon shed a comforting ray, only rushing darkness and the inky channels of the upper air passed by them like a dream.

Southward and eastward they flew. Below them, Kandar guessed, must lie the sea. Ahead, somewhere, lay the land of Akkar. He had learned much of geography since he had left his homeland, and he knew now that Akkar, great and puissant a land though it was, in reality occupied only a small area upon this world.

As though sensing his thoughts, Vrinda of the Nimble Feet said; "We fly for Zafaryque."

"Zafaryque?"

"The continent on which lies your land of Akkar. It is one of the greater continents of this world. There are many things, Akkarian, you do not know. Beyond the enchanted Isle of Histiaea lie other lands, strange, wonderful, altogether lovely lands . . ."

"By Crox! I know!" chimed the hoarse voice of Krak the Mighty in Kandar's skull.

"One day," said Kandar stoutly, "if I live I, too, will visit those lands."

"If you live!" echoed Vrinda of the Silver Hair.

Light grew.

At first Kandar thought it to be another phantom radiance like that that had engulfed the rocky bowl on the Isle of Histiaea. Then he saw the sun's rays shooting up like a greater vision of that blasphemous Hand of Glory. Below the eastern sunrise he saw a long, low band, a bar of darkness, limiting the shining sea.

"See!" cried Vrinda, Felice Estorcis, beloved of gods and men. "Zafaryque!"

The long, powerful wingbeats of the flying dragon drove them surgingly onward.

So involved and caught up with his determination to call on the greater powers had Kandar been that now they had come to his aid, represented to his mortal senses in the person of this gorgeous silver-haired woman riding her flying dragon, he felt his plans fall into pieces. He had no idea of what to do next. What would happen? He remembered the ghastly javelin wound in Elthalee's side, the sword-cut drinking Quantoch's lifeblood. He recalled what the necromancer had wished him to do.

He was going to return to Ferranoz with doctors. He was going to have the best medicine available at his friends' command when they rose from their enchanted sleep.

He had failed! Vrinda would call on her masters to exorcise the spell, and at once the blood would resume pumping out the life from Quantoch and from Elthalee.

Instead of life, he was bringing death!

"Wait!" he screamed into the teeth of the rushing wind.

He tried to explain, babbling to near-incoherence.

Vrinda, Umiris of the Nimble Feet, reassured him with an understanding laugh.

"I understand your fear, Kandar of Ferranoz. But you forget I am also Felice Estorcis, the pain-easer the bringer-forth of new life! If there are friends sore wounded, then I will bring my healing balm. Fret not." Her voice chimed sweetly, melting with savor. "For, Lion of Akkar, I feel a strange yielding to you, a sensation of sympathy I have not felt for any man in a score of thousands of years!"

Krak belched. "By the soft shoulder of sweet Vashtilulu the Buxom! Our Kandar!"

Kandar felt unnecessary.

The woman moved on the seat before him. "There is something strange about you, mortal, some otherliness in you I cannot comprehend. I—perceive, sense, empathize—that you have inner resources impossible to a mortal." She laughed with that reckless outpouring of

117

golden sound. "Come what may, Kandar of Ferranoz, we will save your city and enjoy ourselves mightily afterwards!"

Tosho's whisper breathed in Kandar's mind. "By the shed blood of sweet Majus! You must be careful, Our Kandar!"

Thorblane slanted down. The sea ripened with the dawn. The coastline hardened ahead. Now Kandar could see the irregular outline of the Isle of Sunset like a gilded viol dark against sea glitter.

"The Isle of Sunset!" he exclaimed. "The island to the west of Ferranoz . . . I have seen the sun go down behind that island many and many a time . . ."

"Ferranoz lies just beyond." Wind caught at them. The Lady of the Scaled Cloud exulted in the roistering descent, her silver hair a wild blowing ripple of glory.

Then—then Kandar saw the obscenity staining the sky and plain, saw the fixed and unmoving pall of smoke and the unwavering tongues of static flame.

"Ferranoz!" he shouted, straining. He felt a profound melancholy and at once a blustering riotous uplift of spirits, a devil-be-damned challenge to all the evil forces that sought to destroy Dreaming Ferranoz for sport.

The Gate of Happy Returns lanced up at them from the gray ring walls. In all the sky there was no sign of any wolfling flying ships. Long gone, they had returned with their Garfane pack across the frontiers. Only above the city, half glimpsed among the static smoke-banks, hung the remaining flying ships of the wolf horde.

Vrinda of the Nimble Feet chanted a wild song, a gay lilting challenge. She flung a quick, bright glance back at Kandar where he sat, clutching her lissom waist.

"I have induced the Cloak of Penetration," she cried. Her eyes inflamed him. "Now we can penetrate into the city, live and breathe and move, and remain unaffected by the interlocked enchantments."

"Powerful magic!" came Tosho's squeak. "Already these paramount powers display their strength."

"By the rock-hard kidney of Kragunoth!" roared Krak. "We're in for a fight! I smell it!"

In the air above the city and reducing the flare of the fires to a pallid glare, a radiance grew. A bright, glowing

118

coruscation, spinning, glowing at the center and spitting sparks of lambent fire, the very brilliance of the apparition shocked a clarity into every part of the scene. Vrinda beloved of gods and men turned her face upward. It reflected that divine glare and answered.

"Yes!" cried the woman, her silver hair a blinding mass of white light. "Yes!"

She swung her dazzled green eyes to Kandar. As she spoke to him, the dragon landed in a clap of wings and a spurt of dust. Clumsily, still grasping the sword, Kandar alighted. Vrinda of the Nimble Feet jumped down like a gossamer waft of moonlight.

"Listen to me, Kandar of Ferranoz, for I speak to you as a woman speaks to a man before the shock of battle."

Sobered, tense, Kandar said, "I listen."

"The greater powers whom I serve wish you no ill. They feel friendship for you, and pity. They have no love for those other powers, those evil intelligences, that caught up the wolfling horde of the Garfane and flung them in flying ships upon your city. But, O Lion of Akkar, they never meddle in human affairs without a price being exacted . . ."

"I know, I know," interrupted Kandar. "I have pledged my soul."

"That you have, mortal! But the paramount powers are aloof from the world, impartial, disinterested. You must prove yourself. They have decreed that if you can free your city from the wolflings by your own efforts, you and your countrymen, they will hold all enchantments in check. No sorcery can be employed, either for you or against you. By the strength of your arm and the keenness of your sword must you reclaim your city!"

Kandar swallowed. He nodded.

"I can but fight until I can fight no more, my lady."

She came closer. Her full elastic breasts moved hurriedly. Her scarlet mouth opened softly. Her green eyes drowned him. He was aware of her perfume, of the scent of her silver hair.

"Fight, Kandar of Ferranoz! In your arm's strength, in your sword's skill, lies your hope. Afterwards . . ."

"By Crox!" swore Krak the Mighty. "I'm looking forward to this!"

119

Kandar felt dizzied, unsure. An immortal, the winged messenger of the paramount powers? The harshness of anger in his mouth sweetened to the promise of unnameable adventures. He thought of Angelena, of Elthalee whom he would once again soon see. Yes, he had loved neither of them, and he did not feel love for this glorious woman with the silver hair. But Krak had it right. Swing a good sword and fight a great fight, and after death leave a good name.

With a fixed resolve flaming in him he swung off toward the Gate of Happy Returns.

Quantoch lay where he had been pushed by Kandar's foot.

Quarmeln lay tumbled with the lax body of Elthalee in his arms.

Beyond them the madness began.

As they passed through the gateway, that tingling sensation for a brief moment pinked Kandar all over; then Vrinda of the Nimble Feet brought her Cloak of Penetration into play and the two walked freely in the ensorcelled city.

"The Thaumalogicon," commented Vrinda beloved of gods and men as she knelt by Elthalee, straightening with Kandar's help the body of the girl, putting her arms and legs into a comfortable posture. "I know it as one of the three books of power. You have read in the other two, Kandar, for I am here. But there are many books, many ancient tomes of arcane law. I recommend to your study the *Lobis Maleficarium* and *The Book of Blood*. Had you studied diligently you would not, perhaps, have fallen into the plight in which I found you."

The names of these volumes sent a shudder through Kandar. He busied himself with Quantoch as Vrinda of the Soothing Hands closed Elthalee's wound, her lips moving softly and soundlessly, her face absorbed in her task.

"The Book of Blood!" squeaked Tosho of the small talents. "Thurdur the Cunning possessed the index, but that is all. Even that, when I was his famulus, was kept always chained and locked in an iron chest."

"The princess is again in perfect health," announced Umiris of the Healing Touch, rising with a tinkle of ankle-bells. "Now for the necromancer."

Soon Quantoch, too, had been restored, so that when he regained his senses he would not even realize he had been wounded. Kandar looked toward the palace.

"Before your paramount powers begin, my lady—my family. They, too, may need your ministrations."

The woman nodded. Her green eyes slanted upon Kandar.

"Very well. But you must hurry now. The paramount powers whom I serve will not delay. They have other and pressing business away on the other side of this world. Let us go."

A few yards farther on, Kandar walked past a wolfling. The half-man's snarling lips were ricked back, showing the black gums and the yellow teeth. He was about to drive his sword into the body of an Akkarian infantryman who had just missed in a savage spear lunge. The man's face was sweaty, the drops like marbles of glass on his skin, his eyes desperate, his mouth already forming the wide circle to bring forth his dying scream.

Deliberately, Kandar pushed aside the wolfman's sword blade. Now the infantryman would have time to recover, should be able to bring his spear back for a killing thrust.

Kandar glanced at Vrinda of the Nimble Feet. She had halted and waited for him. At her feet lay a dead captain of the guard, his throat slit from ear to ear.

She shook her head. "I can do nothing for him."

Kandar took the slain captain's armor and clothed his own nakedness. He buckled up the corselet straps. Now he felt a little more ready for the coming fight. He picked up the dead man's sword. "No!" said Vrinda of the Silver Hair. "It is my masters' express ruling. You must fight with the great sword you bear. Otherwise . . ." She smiled at him. "Why carry it?"

"Why indeed!" grumbled Kandar.

He hushed Krak the Mighty's outraged bellow. They continued walking toward the palace. Now, more and more, Kandar positioned the combatants. Here he removed an arrow from the bow of a half-man, an arrow aimed at the heart of a struggling infantryman of the guard. There he pushed a soldier's shield across properly to deflect a stabbing wolfling sword.

"Training!" he grunted. "Why will they swing their shields around instead of covering their bodies with them?"

They came to the intersection where the avenue leading from the Gate of Happy Returns crossed the Imperial Way. At once he glanced up toward the palace. Immobile fire and smoke sprouted from it in a dozen places. All along the Imperial Way lay scattered bodies of wolflings and charioteers; he recognized with a pang the accouterments of his brother's squadron.

What he could do to aid the warriors of his city he did. But time was running short, time, which he had thought to be impossible of consuming in this time-static ensorcellment. Vrinda of the Silver Hair urged him to hurry. Quickly he ran from group to group, re-arranging, repositioning, organizing. There would be many surprised wolflings when the stasis shattered.

He realized as he worked that he could do all these things only through the intervention of the paramount powers. They held in check the opposing forces of the evil intelligences who sported with Fair Ferranoz.

"Hurry!" urged Umiris of the Winged Feet, the woman Vrinda, running on, her silver hair an aureole of light. "The powers I serve chafe at the delay! Their interest weakens! Already the evil intelligences clamor and struggle and seek to overthrow them! Make haste, mortal!"

Quickly and ever more quickly Kandar ran along the Imperial Way. He did what he could. Then he was bounding up the long flight of steps to the palace, past tumbled bodies of charioteers, wolfmen, archers, racing up toward his home.

On the topmost step his father, Pandin Heliodōtus, God-Emperor of all Akkar, stood in regal dignity, clad in his war harness, his true sword Peveril in his hand. His face showed gray with weariness and disillusion and despair.

Kandar darted forward.

"Sheldion!" He cried. "My brother!"

The Prince Sheldion lay all asprawl, the blood in a sinuous, stilled bubble that welled from his neck. At his side lay the tough gnarled body of his driver, Tojas.

"Vrinda of the Opulent Charms!" called Kandar in a gust of dismay. "Umiris of the Soothing Hands! My brother, the Prince Sheldion—"

"Hush, hush, mortal!" she chided him. Swiftly, with a chiming of ankle-bells she knelt, began to work her healing beneficence on the body of the Crown Prince.

When Sheldion showed no sign of that javelin-driven wound she looked up, smiling. "The interlocked enchantments end, Kandar of Ferranoz! Your city once again enters this time-stream. Be ready. Gird yourself for battle. This is what you have sold your soul to accomplish."

She moved aside, bent above an archer of the guard, began to soothe away the ghastly wound in his side. The light above the city pierced in downward-spearing lines through the smoke. A strange piercing thrilling began in the air. The marbles of the palace shook, the air thrummed with power, the air sucked and whooshed as though spun in the eye of a cyclone.

Grimly, Kandar battled that wind, strode to stand with naked brand before the thin line of archers and charioteers.

He used both hands on Koztivkure. He knew he could not swing that awesome blade for very long. But while he could, he would fight on for Dreaming Ferranoz.

The enchantments ended.

The city jerked into life and motion and noise.

The ballista in the tower across from the towerless gardens bright with funley-flowers clanged, and the great rock flew.

All over the city the enchantment-supported ships of the wolf horde fell from the sky, fell like discarded chips from the sawmill, fell to crash in red ruin on the pavements of Fair Ferranoz.

Noise and clash of battle resounded hideously all through the streets and avenues.

But now—but now!

Everywhere the men of Akkar, seeing that disastrous collapse of the wolf ships, took heart. They guessed that enchantment had at last come to their aid. With savage force they burst upon the stunned ranks of the wolflings. In a wild melee of clashing blades and darting javelins, of thrusting spears and skimming arrows, they pressed the dismayed half-men back. Gray-gristle bodies fell, to be trampled beneath bronze-studded sandals. Blood flowed darkly upon the age-old marbles of Fair Ferranoz, but now that blood spouted from gray wolfling bodies.

On the steps of the palace, with the wolflings hesitating in their surge upward, Pandin Heliodotus stood proudly, his true blade Peveril a blinding shaft of light. To him rallied the charioteers and the bowmen.

All had experienced a subtle but profound shock, as though their hearts had, for a moment, stopped beating.

Gnarled Tojas rose, and as he staggered up, so the Prince Sheldion, too, rose. Alight with the discovery that he had not, after all, been wounded, he raced to his father.

He saw Kandar.

"How in the name of Lord Helios—?"

"There is no time now, Sheldion. Right glad am I to see you, brother! Now, for the sake of Dreaming Ferranoz and all of Fair Akkar, we must fight!"

And Kandar of Ferranoz leaped down the palace steps.

Straight into the upsurging ranks of the wolflings he plunged. Koztivkure became a flaming brand of destruction. Keenly the edge bit. Deeply the point drank of alien blood. Whirled about his head like a discus of living light, the great sword lopped heads and arms, carved gray bodies, slashed through brass-studded black armor as a heated blade slides through fat. Silently, all his breath pent for the wielding of Krak's mighty blade, Kandar hewed his way down the steps.

With a triumphant shout, Sheldion, Tojas, the charioteers and the archers leaped after him.

Together, the men of Ferranoz drove the wolflings before them.

Desperately the wolf horde fought. Each gray half-man knew he must fight or die, for there would be no flying ships for his escape.

A clamor arose as Kandar reached the marbles of the Imperial Way. Infantrymen of the guard, in a compact double line, had been cleaving their way into the reeling ranks of half-men. Suddenly Akkarian swords clattered to the marble. Soldiers reeled back.

With an abrupt shock Kandar saw a wriggling mass of black vipers coiling about each Akkarian's shield. As he watched, a basket-sized clump of snakes materialized in the air before him, descended to engulf Koztivkure.

"Magic!" he shouted, high and angry. He swung about,

shaking the snakes free, cutting black bodies into chops.

Umiris of the Nimble Feet ran down the steps. Her face showed consternation. The men of Ferranoz stumbled back, screaming. The wolflings chirred their triumph and surged forward, swords and spears lifted.

"You said there would be no enchantments!" Kandar screamed.

"I promised—" she called over the noise to him. "I gave the word of an immortal—my masters must—"

A glow descended all about them. Lightnings flashed. Thunder rolled. The snakes disappeared. All about them in an eerie light a kind of diaphanous veil of light motes fell. Great winds tore across the city. Vast sheets of lightning pulsed and crackled.

Over the city an immeasurably vaster battle was being fought. Intelligence against intelligence, power against power, invisible, omnipotent, the opposing beings clashed in enchanted combat.

Kandar brandished Koztivkure.

"Forward!" he shouted. "Attack! Now we drive every last misbegotten wolfling from Dreaming Ferranoz!"

With a great shout and renewed hope the men of Akkar swung their weapons against the wolf horde. Down the steps, along the Imperial Way, picking up more and more men as they advanced, the Akkarians forged a path of steel and blood.

Koztivkure became as light as a rapier in Kandar's hands. At his side, laughing, reckless, a glowing force, Vrinda of the Silver Hair urged him on.

"For me, Kandar of Ferranoz! Fight for me!"

"Aye!" he gasped, slicing a screeching half-man in two. "Aye, Umiris the bewitching! For Ferranoz and Akkar—and then for you!"

Along the Imperial Way they fought. Down to the harbor where the wolflings plunged into the morning-glittering sea. Archers stood on the quays and jetties to pick off swimming gray heads.

Soon no wolfling was left alive in Cleansed Ferranoz.

"By the sinews of Kragunoth's strong right arm!" boomed a riotous voice in Kandar's skull. "By Crox! I enjoyed that!"

Kandar became aware that all through the battle Krak

had been roaring and bellowing away, urging him on, counseling him, teaching him the tricks of Koztivkure.

And Tosho, too, Tosho the Fox, had been caught up in that bedlam of excitement, had been squeaking encouragement.

"You have won all, through the blessed deliverance of the shed blood of sweet Majus! Through his intercession have we conquered. We humbly give thanks."

"I'll second that, Tosho of the not-so-small talents," said Kandar, laughing. He leaned on his sword. His body felt light, free, not yet the receptacle of the pains he would soon feel in reaction to the battle. He was splashed from head to heels in blood.

Quantoch, Quarmeln and Elthalee walked toward him. From the Imperial Way, Pandin Heliodotus, mounted on Sheldion's own chariot with the four milk-white steeds frothing and straining, galloped up, with King Shamrath crouched on the tailboard. Prince Sheldion, blood-stained like his brother, and Tojas joined them.

"It is over!" marveled Sheldion.

"And you have become a man," said Pandin Heliodotus to Kandar. He looked with fond eyes on this scapegrace son.

"Oh, Kandar! My beloved!" sobbed Elthalee. She ran to Kandar and was caught up in his arms, the blood dabbling her gown. He felt the strength in his limbs. He felt the pride of these, his people, around him.

A shadow fell athwart the marble.

"Have you forgotten, Kandar of Ferranoz, foresworn to the paramount powers?"

Vrinda of the Silver Hair stood gazing at him, her green eyes alight now with fresh conquests. Elthalee looked at her and shivered. She grasped Kandar more tightly.

"What . . .? Who is *she*, my beloved?"

He put Elthalee gently from him, a poignant pang of remembrance at the way he had put Angelena from him on the enchanted Isle of Histiaea stabbing him mercilessly.

"I . . ." he said. How could he explain?

"My winged wonder of the sun awaits us, Kandar—my own!"

The cruelty of it all tortured Kandar. He had won, and

126

yet he had lost irredeemably.

"Hear me, mortals!" chimed the winged messenger of the immortal powers. "Prince Kandar of Ferranoz has pledged his soul for the sake of you and your city. No longer may he stay within the gray walls of Ferranoz."

"No!" gasped Elthalee, her face ghastly.

"The price he must pay for the help of the greater powers is just. The gesture he has made to save the city must be pure, and must be seen to be pure. He cannot benefit personally. He must not set foot again in Ferranoz, not before at least thrice seven years have passed. His actions were not self-seeking. Now he must go forth, his soul at the command of the paramount powers, whom I serve, at their behest. His soul is forfeit. Come, Kandar of Ferranoz! Say your farewells. Let us begone!"

How to say goodbye? How explain? Was there anything left to explain?

He kissed Elthalee; he looked his father in the eye and received his benediction, his secret sign of blessing; he embraced his brother Sheldion; he took farewells of Quantoch and his twin brother Quarmeln. He looked about on Dreaming Ferranoz, the city he had saved at such a price.

"It is good," he said, with humble resignation.

The winged dragon Thorblane waited. Up to the saddle he mounted, clasping the lush body of Vrinda of the Silver Hair, the great sword Koztivkure slung around his neck and dangling down his back.

As the winged dragon rose with a clash of scarlet pinions, he looked down. He was leaving all his life there—yet Angelena waited in far-off Lodge Ascapard. There were books of thaumaturgical lore to be found and read. Life promised its compensations.

There was a world waiting to be explored.

And . . .

"You have done well, Our Kandar. By the shed blood of sweet Majus, thrice seven years will quickly pass."

And . . .

"By the bounteous bottom of sweet Vashtilulu the Buxom! I'm looking forward to this, Our Kandar!"

SWORD, SORCERY AND SAVAGERY
IN KING ARTHUR'S TIME

THE GREEN MAN
by Henry Treece

"A bloody, furious tale colored by barbaric pagan
rites."—*Publishers' Weekly*

"A magnificently full-blooded picture of a glorious,
little-known age."—*The American News*

"Full of legendary heroes and their passions, goals
and intrigues."—*Beaumont (Tex.) Journal*

(55-752, 95¢)